NOBODY'S ANGEL

Thomas McGuane

NOBODY'S ANGEL

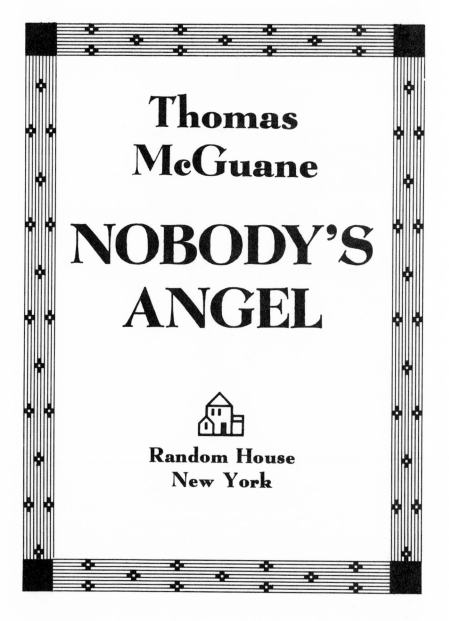

Random House
New York

A small portion of this work appeared in the Spring 1980 edition
of *Triquarterly*, and the May 1979 edition of *Rocky Mountain Magazine*.

*Grateful acknowledgment is made to the following for
permission to reprint previously published material:*

Warner Bros. Music: Two lines of lyric from
"Jack Daniels If You Please" by David Allen Coe. © 1978 by
Warner-Tamerlane Publishing Corp. All rights reserved. Used by permission.

Library of Congress Cataloging in Publication Data

McGuane, Thomas.
Nobody's angel.

I. Title.
PS3563.A3114N6   813'.54   81-13885
ISBN 0-394-52264-8   AACR2
ISBN 0-394-70565-3 (pbk.)

Manufactured in the United States of America

2 4 6 8 9 7 5 3

FIRST EDITION

This book is for my beloved Laurie,
still there when the storm passed

"I love hell. I can't wait to get back."

—MALCOLM LOWRY

NOBODY'S ANGEL

— ❖ 1 ❖ —

YOU WOULD HAVE TO CARE ABOUT THE COUNTRY. NOBODY
had been here long enough and the Indians had been very
thoroughly kicked out. It would take a shovel to find
they'd ever been here. In the grasslands that looked so
whorled, so cowlicked from overhead, were the ranches.
And some of these ranches were run by men who thought
like farmers and who usually had wives twice their size.
The others were run by men who thought like cowboys
and whose wives, more often than not, were their own size
or smaller, sometimes quite tiny. The farmer-operators
were good mechanics and packed the protein off the land.
The cowboys had maybe a truck and some saddle horses;
and statistics indicate that they had an unhealthy depen-
dence on whiskey. They were not necessarily violent nor
necessarily uneducated. Their women didn't talk in the
tiny baby voices of the farmer-operator wives nor in the
beautician rasp of the town wives. The cowboys might
have gotten here last week or just after the Civil War, and
they seemed to believe in what they were doing; though
they were often very lazy white men.

The town in the middle of this place was called Deadrock, a modest place of ten thousand souls, originally
named for an unresolved battle between the Army and the
Assiniboin—Deadlock—but renamed Deadrock out of

some sad and irresolute boosterism meant to cure an early-day depression. To many people Deadrock was exactly the right name; and in any case it stuck. It was soon to be a major postcard.

Patrick Fitzpatrick lived on a ranch thirty-one miles outside of town. He was a forth-generation cowboy outsider, an educated man, a whiskey addict and until recently a professional soldier. He was thirty-six years old. He was in good shape; needed some crown work but that was about it.

❖ 2 ❖

THE YARD LIGHT ERECT UPON ITS WOOD STANCHION THREW down a yellow faltering glow infinitely chromatic falling through the China willow to the ground pounded up against the house by the unrepentantly useless horses. Patrick Fitzpatrick glided under the low branches on his mare as the band circled into the corral for salt and grain and water and the morning's inspection for cracked hooves, lameness, splints, bowed tendons, lice, warbles, wire cuts, ulcerated eyes, wolf teeth, spavin, gravel, founder and worms.

Near the light's edge the dogs watched him pass: Cole Younger, yellow, on his back, all four legs dangling, let his eyelids fall open upside down; Alba, black, in the sub-shadow of mountain ash, ready to run; Zip T. Crow, brindle, jaw alight on parallel front legs, considered starting a stampede with his hyena voice. Thinking finally of the consequences, he fell to dreaming as the last horse, a yearling running at an angle, jog-trotted into the corral to drink in the creek alongside the other shadowy horses deployed as regularly as a picket line. Zip T. Crow slunk over behind some relic of a walking cultivator and dropped into its confused shadows like a shy insurrectionist. This was the day to ride up to the airplane.

IN VERY EARLY SPRING BEFORE THE CREEKS FLOODED, BEFORE the first bridges washed away and the big river turned dark, before the snow was gone from the rugged shadows and the drowned livestock tumbled up in the brushy banks, Patrick found the airplane with his binoculars—a single ripped glimmer of fuselage visible a matter of hours before the next flurry concealed it for another month but not before Patrick had memorized the deep-blue ultramontane declivity at the top of the fearsome mountain and begun speculating if in May he could get a horse through the last ten thousand yards of deadfall and look into the pilot's eyes. Patrick was the son of a dead pilot.

Then in May Patrick walked up the endless sloping nose and saw the pilot quite clearly. He climbed past him to the copilot's seat and found fractured portions of granite, parts of the mountain that had poured like grapeshot through the fuselage clear into the tail section, leaving the copilot in innumerable pieces, those pieces gusseted in olive nylon, and the skin of the aircraft blood-sprayed as in a cult massacre. Farther aft in the tapering shape where the beating spring sun shone on the skin of the plane and where viscera trailed off in straps, fastening and instruments, it stank. Arms raised in uniform, the pilot seemed the image of a man in receipt of a fatal sacrament. The oxygen hose was torn away, and beyond the nautiloid effigy, Patrick could see his mare grazing on the alpine slope. Unable to differentiate flesh and electronics, he was avoiding the long-held notion that his father had died like a comet, igniting in the atmosphere, an archangelic semaphore more dignified than death itself. For Patrick, a year had begun. The inside of the plane showed him that life doesn't just always drag on.

PATRICK LEFT THE SIDEWALK THROUGH THE DOOR BETWEEN the two angled windows. It was cold, but when he hung his coat inside and glanced onto the street, it looked like summer. Purest optics. There was a stock truck parked at the hotel with two saddled horses in back facing opposite directions. Many saddle horses spend the day parked in front of a bar, heads hung in sleep. Can't get good help anymore, Patrick thought. Even if you could, who wants to tell people what to do?

Two steps up at the poker table was an old man with a diamond willow cane pushing chips onto the green felt. There was a belton setter at his feet, two strangers and a girl dealing cards. Not strangers, but he couldn't remember their names.

"Afternoon, Patrick," said the old man, whose name was Carson. That was his first name.

One stranger said, "Hello, Captain"—Patrick had been in the Army—and the other said, "How's the man?" Classmates with forgotten faces. But Patrick was rather graceful under these conditions, and by the time he'd gone through the room, the setter was asleep again, the players were smiling and the girl dealing was reading his name off the back of his belt.

The bar was nearly empty, populated solely by that handful of citizens who can drink in the face of sun blazing through the windows. Patrick ordered his whiskey, knocked it back and reconnoitered. Whiskey, he thought, head upstairs and do some good.

He called, "Thanks so much!" to the bar girl, put down his money and left. It was hard to leave a place where God was at bay.

He walked all the way to the foot of Main, straight toward the mountain range, crossed the little bridge over the clear overflow ditch and went into a prefabricated home without knocking. The windows were covered with shades, and once his eyes accustomed themselves to the poor light, he could see the prostitutes on the couch watching an intelligent interview show, the kind in which Mr. Interlocutor is plainly on amphetamines, while his subjects move in grotesque slow motion. They were dealing with the fetus's right to life. On the panel were four abortionists, five anti-abortionists and a livid nun with the temper of an aging welterweight.

"Hello, girls."

"Hello, Patrick."

"No game on?"

"College basketball. We're watching this fetus deal."

"Anybody make a profit?"

"Loretta did."

Loretta, a vital brunette with tangled hair and a strong, clean body, beamed. She said, "Trout fishermen. Doctors, I think. One had a penlight. He said he always checked for lesions. I said clap. He said among other things. I said four- to ten-day incubation. He says which book are you reading. I said I don't read books, I watch TV. So he gets in there with this penlight. I could've swatted him."

"Free checkup," said Patrick. "Look at the good side of things."

"Who's winning?" Loretta asked. She came from Deadrock, looked like a nice farm girl.

Deirdre, from Great Falls, always literal, said, "The fetus." This nun was packing the mail.

Patrick asked if they were betting. They said no. He said that as he was a Catholic, he would kick in the set if the fetus lost.

"There's a Catholic," said Tana as the camera isolated the apoplectic nun shouting the word "*Sacred!*"

"I've seen better ones," said Patrick.

"Well, there's one, is all," she said doggedly.

Andrea, the young, bright blond, was from the High Line. She said, "I was with this rancher on his place. He wanted to go again. All the lights went out. I said that's Rural Electrification for you. He said that's Montana Power. I said well, I can't see nothin. He said it's hydroelectric. It comes off the grid, out of Columbia Falls. So I said what's the deal? Do we go again? He said not if I can't see. And just then, like God was on my side, the power came back on and I doubled down for fifty bucks. Thank you, Montana Power! Thank you, Columbia Falls!"

"Jesus," Patrick said. "That nun is going to blow her stack." He was staring at the screen.

"She's no help to the fetus team," said Loretta. The moderator kept saying, "*Sister! Sister!*" but nothing could slow her tirade, which continued to feature the word "*Sacred!*" repeated at very high volume.

"I'm glad I don't have any money on this one," said Patrick. Andrea got up and went to the kitchen to make

iced tea. Loretta, from Deadrock, had gone to grammar
school with Patrick, had been a medical secretary, then
been not quite happy with that and tried prostitution, a
respected job in Montana because of its long utility during
the settlement of that region. Loretta's rural good looks
made her prosper, particularly among visiting sportsmen.

Deirdre, from Great Falls, said, "That nun could use
some eye shadow." Deirdre was best with closing-time
stumblebums. Patrick asked Loretta if he could have a
word with her privately.

The two went into the kitchen as Patrick fought back a
little tingle. Loretta hiked herself up on the counter and
Patrick sat in a ladder-back chair. There were coffee cans
on a low shelf, each labeled with one of the girls' names;
and in front of every can was a kitchen timer. The cans
held each night's earnings and the clocks foiled dawdling
or inappropriate enthusiasm.

"Loretta," said Patrick. "You're prettier than you were
at homecoming." Only an officer. She'd actually gone
downhill.

"I've got a better life now. When did you get back?"

"Not too long ago. In the winter."

"You home to stay?"

"Trying to be. It'll depend on what I can get going.
We're still running pairs and I've got a few outside horses
to break, if I can remember how. I guess my grandfather
has just had to pick up whoever he could. So a lot of
things have kind of gone downhill."

"He had that one Indian for quite a while. Supposed to
have been a good hand."

"What Indian?"

"He was, you know, a friend of Mary's, the way I had
it." Mary was Patrick's sister.

"Well, Mary is why I'm here."

"What's the trouble?"

"No trouble. I just can't find her. I mean, I thought you might know."

"She got out of this work a long time ago, Pat. The Indian is the best way to find her I know. He was supposed to be real different. Used to shark pool at the Corral, just take everybody's money and never say a word. You know, an *Indian*."

"Well, I'm not going to go hunt her down or anything. But if you see her, tell her I'm home."

"I sure will."

"Boy, you look good, Loretta."

"More!" She put on her "It Girl" smile and spun on her toes.

Patrick walked over to the can labeled "Loretta," wound the clock in front of it and turned it loose real slow.

"Gives me a vicarious thrill," he said. She waved as he went out the door into the sunlight that bounced from the high walls of granite around the town.

❖ **5** ❖

PATRICK WAS TICKING OFF OBLIGATIONS. HE WALKED BACK outside under the heartless blue sky. He was searching for his grandfather, who had left the ranch early that morning. Patrick feared a binge. But as he had just left the Army and was not yet used to being home, he was rather like someone out of stir, trying to establish a pattern in a new world. For example, this morning after feeding the horses, he had thought very seriously about moving to

Madrid. He had learned Spanish at the Monterey language school, but the Army made him a tank captain in Germany. Nonetheless, he often daydreamed of an ancient walk-up in Castile with a stone kitchen, a cook he could afford and a stream of interesting characters who could understand that what had begun as scholarship had precipitated him into cold-war mongery, *not* a desire to drive a bulletproof dump truck on the East German line. Patrick had read widely, could break horses and did not, as yet, live in Spain. In any case, he would never reveal his love for the tank. He was tall, single, had lost his father and looked after a grandfather who now drank too much. Patrick drank a little too much. His father had been a test pilot for Boeing. His mother remarried in California. Lately, Patrick was having trouble answering letters, especially the prying ones from the family about the finances of the ranch, which were precarious; and with each arrival of the mail it had become a real Mexican standoff between hiring a secretary and embarking for Castile.

Angled on the corner of Big Horn and Main was the Part-Time Bar, where Patrick went to have a George Dickel and water as a way of staking the place out for his grandfather. The Part-Time was an old-timers' favorite. The homemade soup there took a little of the edge off the binges and sustained anyone hungry in search of company. This hunger struck at all hours.

Patrick walked in and it was busy. He surveyed the room; no sign of his grandfather. At the bar many aging backs hunched in concealment.

"Anybody seen the old man?"

About fifteen nopes.

Patrick got his whiskey at the bar, sat down in the row of older faces and thought: This is the kind of place that makes you want to grow old, just sit here and eavesdrop.

Down the bar:

"I was born in 1904."

"Here?"

"Evidently."

Cigarette smoke moved horizontally toward the EXIT-TELEPHONE-REST ROOM sign.

Every time someone entered, "What d'ya know?" in a hearty voice; and the reply: "Not much." The "o" in "know" carrying the drawn-out local dipthong.

Patrick sipped in deep contentment. Underneath the murmur of conversation and easy laughter was the continuous slap of plastic chips from the poker game in the corner.

An elderly man next to Patrick in a John B. Stetson hat and blue suspenders said, "Colder it gets, the more a guy'll notice." He stared fixedly at the commemorative bottles. A pretty girl in a blue sweater dealt poker and in a firm voice repeated the rules. The new players feared her.

"Fifty cents to a buck on the deal and before the flop. There's a three-raise limit on each round, no cutting. Twenty bucks to buy in."

The old man next to Patrick was adjusting his butt on the stool, improving his angle for a conversation. The bartender shot past to the glass-and-wood cooler that displayed five kinds of beer at knee level. Patrick tried to read the farm-auction poster from twenty feet; thought, Used to could do that.

A voice from the corner: "Can't draw no goddamned clubs."

The bartender collected more orders—Sunny Brook,

Cabin Still, Old Grand Dad, Canadian Mist, another George Dickel for Patrick.

"Hungry?"

"No," said Patrick.

"We got three kinds of beef jerky—King B, Big Slim and Rawhide Ranch."

"I don't think so."

"Plus beer nuts and smoked almonds."

"Who shot that six-pointer?"

"I did, Pat. Right after Korea."

The old man asked the bartender, "What bets've I got?"

"You got the Pirates and the Tigers."

"Buck a square?"

"Yup."

"What kind of cigars you got?"

"Everything from White Owl to R. G. Dun."

"Gimme an R. G. Dun."

Patrick thought that in a moment the old man would tell him where his grandfather was; he was warming up and didn't want to be a squealer. Patrick pointed to a bottle of Hiram Walker chocolate-mint liqueur and asked, "Ever try that?"

"No."

The old man knew Patrick knew. He was going to play it silent. Down the bar a heavy woman in her sixties squinted and started describing commemorative bottles in a lungful of Lucky Strike smoke: "Illinois Gladiola Festival, a 'Ducks Unlimited,' an Australian koala bear, Indian chief, Abraham Lincoln, the Kentucky Derby, Am Vets, a telephone—"

"Barkeep, what's it say on that model train?"

" 'Jupiter.' Says just 'Jupiter.' "

"I don't know what in the hell that means. Why don't somebody scrape that junk down from offa there?"

The old man pivoted to Patrick. "Your grandfather is trying out for a movie."

"He what?"

"Read the poster on the inside of the door."

CASTING CALL
for HONDO'S LAST MOVE, *a feature film.*

WANTED
Men, women and children for bit players, extras, et cetera.

ALSO NOTE
In order to reflect the hardships endured in the West in the 1880's, we would especially welcome the physically eccentric, those with permanent physical injuries, such as scars, missing teeth, broken limbs, broken noses, missing limbs, etc.

CONTACT
Arnold Duxbury, Casting Coordinator, Room 115–17, Murray Hotel. Interviews commence daily at 10:00 A.M.

Patrick thought, The old bugger has scars, missing teeth and evidence of a broken nose. That is where we shall find him. One episode too many of Wagon Train, dog-food ads masquerading as life.

Rooms 115–17 were, respectively, reception, waiting room and Duxbury. There was a considerable lineup of the maimed. The worst was a five-year-old boy whose pet wildcat had recently clawed out his eyeball. He wore an oozing patch and steered his head around, trying to figure out what he was doing there. His mother, a telephone operator who moonlighted at the Tempo Supper Club, respected her son's injury enough to bark "*No cuts!*" at Patrick when he tried to move up the line and look for his grandfather. The mother indignantly steered the little boy forward by the arm, and Patrick sheepishly got at the end while the halt, lame and maimed glowered at him, thinking, It's the bloody tank captain from the Heart Bar Ranch, trying to throw his weight around. But the sound of crutches and labored breathing grew behind him, and soon he stood at the desk of Marion Garland, who said, "What brings you to the geek show?" *Streets of Laredo* poured from a neighboring room.

"I'm looking for my grandfather—"

"What's your grandfather's name?"

"Frank Fitzpatrick."

"Francis X?"

"Yes."

"He's with Mr. Duxbury now."

"I'll just go in and get him."

"That's not our procedure—"

"It is now."

Patrick walked past her into Arnold Duxbury's office. Duxbury was a youthful forty. Every single thing he had on was denim, including his boots, which Patrick did not think was possible; treated rubber, perhaps.

Francis X. Fitzpatrick was showing a mule kick by taking off his pants. Duxbury explained that that would be unnecessary, as we were dealing with family entertainment. The crooked upper thigh was the old man's trump card and he wouldn't take no for an answer. Finally Duxbury said, "Hey, relax, you're in the movie." The old man shot his sleeves confidently.

"On the basis of what?" he demanded.

"The nose and your age."

"Well, write my name down."

"I already did."

"I'll see you on the set," said the old man, fastening his trousers. "Y'know what I mean? You better spelt my name correct."

"Come on, Grandpa," said Patrick. "I need you at the place. You mind?"

Duxbury and Garland signed up eighty-seven permanently injured Americans for *Hondo's Last Move* and returned to Los Angeles. The film was already in trouble; the distributor was thinking of pulling out to do something more in the Space line, as Westerns were beginning to show signs of what he called in a *Variety* interview "metal fatigue."

Nobody ever saw Duxbury and Garland again. As it turned out, Patrick's grandfather would never quite get over it. His heart was on a movie poster, however close to the bottom. There were still small wings on his shoes.

❖ 6 ❖

PATRICK GAVE HIS GRANDFATHER A GOOD LEAD, THEN GOT IN the Ford and started home. The yellow truck shot along the river road against the amphitheater in the Absaroka range between Case Creek and Sheep Creek. A summer storm hung in the deepest pass above the truck, and lightning volleyed in silence. Patrick glanced at his knuckles, looked up, dodged a pothole, admired a hawk circling in a thermal against the limited storm now evaporating like steam on glass. The truck sucked down into the creek bottom. The storm dematerialized and left the hawk in empty blue.

Patrick stopped at the calving shed a mile below the house and played Ornette Coleman on the machine, wondered why Ornette always had a white bass player and why he made you think so hard. Patrick decided that because Ornette was such a thorough master of bebop, he knew a white man could be expected to play melodic bass and not worry too much about time. Was Ornette as clever as the Yardbird? Why was there not a statue of Charlie Parker in Washington? When Patrick thought of Ornette Coleman running an elevator in Los Angeles with a roomful of scores and his mother sending him food from Texas, he developed grave doubts about the District of Columbia.

Patrick daydreamed on with unimpeded high energy. Lenin's girl friend Inessa Armand died in 1920 of typhus in the North Caucasus. Patrick read that in a Mexican comic book while preparing for flight to Castile. He read that in the vague interior light of a high-speed American tank in Germany. He was a security measure. He liked whiskey. Most of the other security measures preferred pharmaceuticals. With their dilated pupils and langorous movements, they were there to help save the West from the East, should the occasion arise. Patrick felt they had already gone East. But then, he was a captain, and being an officer had slowly sunk against the grain until finally, strangely, he was actually an Army captain, if you could see around the matter of the Mexican comic books.

I will work the claybank mare. She has taken to running through the bridle. She does not fall off to the right as well as she does to the left. I want her to drag, lock down and turn around when she needs to. We are not trying to make trail horses. We are not leading a string of dudes to a photo view of Scissorbill Peak.

Next to the barn a cat ran through three shadows without touching the sunlight, then emerged triumphant in the glare, mouse crosswise in its hard domestic mouth. After a motionless instant the cat started toward the green lawn and the house, where, in front of the sink, it would leave the minute head and vermiculate insides of the mouse.

The horses, maybe twenty head, were all in a pod on the far side of the corral, shaded by cottonwoods. Wild rose bushes grew right to the poles, and the sides of the corral were like a tall hedge, illuminated by the pale-pink blossoms. The claybank mare was in the center of the band, nearer the side of the corral, really; and as Patrick closed the gate to walk toward the horses, the mare, butt toward him, shifted her head slightly for better rear-angle vision—out of a very real sense that it was she who was going up to the pasture with Patrick and not the other roughly nineteen. She looked like a shoplifter.

In this bunch there were no kickers, and so Patrick murmured his way gently through the big bodies, feeling their heat and watching the quizzical movement of the claybank mare's head and ears. Some of the horses kept sleeping, the good old saddle horses, lower lips trembling in massive dreams, one or another rear foot tipped up, weight transferred from muscle to ligament in that horse magic of standing sleep; one or two craning, ignorant yearlings, and Patrick's hand touched the mare's flank, which twitched involuntarily, as though he'd shuffled across a carpet and given her a flicker of static electricity. He said softly, "Hey, now," as he moved toward her head. "Care to go with me to Spain? Little walk-up deal with a cool stone kitchen?" And he had her haltered, turned around and headed for the gate, the mare flopping her feet along, knowing she was going to school.

Patrick brushed her thoroughly, watching the early light go through her coat. Claybank and grulla were his preferred colors; claybank, just like it sounded, a blur away from a copper dun, or a copper dun that had been rolling in alkali dust, then run for a mile until the color started through once more. *Grulla* was Spanish for blue heron. Grullas had better feet than claybanks and were said to stand the sun well. This far north it didn't matter. Patrick irrationally believed that anything dun, claybank or buckskin had more cow sense.

He saddled the mare with two Mexican blankets. You had to kind of rub the blankets up onto her or she'd try to pull the hitching rack out of the ground. She was young. And when he pitched the saddle up on her, he held the cinch, girth and billets so that nothing would slap and start her pulling back. Today he tried her in a grazing bit to get her nose out a little; he had been riding her on a higher-ported bit, and she was collecting her head too much, tucking it up like some fool show horse from California. Patrick liked them with their faces out, looking around, their feet under them, not like something in front of the supermarket that takes quarters.

This mare was searching for a reason to be a bronc, as perhaps they all were; so Patrick walked her in a figure eight to untrack her, stood in one stirrup for a moment, then crawled on. By your late thirties the ground has begun to grow hard. It grows harder and harder until the day that it admits you.

Then a half mile in deep grass and early light, time for a smart young horse to have a look around, scare up some meadowlarks, salivate on the copper mouthpiece, get a little ornery bow in her back and get rid of it. Patrick changed his weight from stirrup to stirrup, felt her compensate, then stopped her. She fidgeted a moment, waited, then let the tension go out of her muscles. He moved her out again to the right. All she gave him was her head; so he stopped her, drew her nose each way nearly to his boot, then made a serpentine track across the pasture, trying to get a gradual curve throughout her body in each of her turns. The rowels on his spurs were loose enough that they chinked with her gaits. Patrick used spurs like a pointing finger, pressing movement into a shape, never striking or gouging. And horseback, unlike any other area of his life, he never lost his temper, which, in horsemen, is the final mark of the amateur.

Patrick broke the mare out into a long trot, dropping her back each time she tried to move into a lope. She made one long buck out of irritation, then leveled off like a pacer eating up ground and slowly rotating the cascading hills, to Patrick's happy observation. I love this scene. It has no booze or women in it, he rejoiced.

He set the mare down twice, liked her stops, then blew her out for half a mile, the new fence going past his eyes like a filament of mercury, and let her jog home while he told her continuously how wonderful she was, what a lovely person she was becoming.

Black coffee and a morning breeze through the paper. Martinsdale Hutterites had recalled three hundred contaminated chickens. Cowboys for Christ was having a benefit. Billings fireman captured with three pounds of methamphetamines. Poplar man shot to death in Wolf Point; Bureau of Indian Affairs investigator and tribal police arrested two men as yet unnamed. Half million in felonious cattle defaults. Formerly known as bum deals, thought Patrick. A new treatment center for compulsive gamblers. Lives shattered by slot machines. Wanted or for sale: TV stand, green-broke horse, ladies' western suits, four-drawer blond dresser, harvest-gold gas range, three box-trained kittens, nonleak laundry tubs, top dollar for deer and elk hides, Brown Swiss, presently milking, Phoenix or Yuma to share gas. When Patrick's father went down testing an airplane, fast enough that its exterior skin glowed at night from the friction of the air, the hurtling pulp which had been his father and the navigator and which had passed through the intricate molecular confusion of an exploding aircraft at its contact with eastern Oregon, the paper identified him as Patrick Fitzpatrick of Deadrock, Montana, and the navigator as Del Andrews of Long Beach, California. Great space was given to the model of the aircraft and speculation about a declared salvage value. As so many people have had to wonder, Patrick thought, if my father is dead, how can I be alive? In this way Patrick lost much of his own fear of death. The crash had provoked none of the questions usual to accidental death. There was nothing to identify.

Patrick's grandfather walked into the kitchen, opened the refrigerator, stared about at the contents, settled for a handful of radishes and sat down.

"What's the cattle market doing?"

"Haven't had the radio on," said Patrick. "Somebody sold a bunch of bred heifers in Billings yesterday for a twenty-seven-hundred-dollar average."

"Bred how?"

"Shoshone or Chandelier Forever, forgot which. You want me to make you some breakfast?"

"I can rustle."

"Here, sit down. What do you want?"

"Couple of soft-boiled eggs."

Patrick started getting them ready. "In Europe there'd be these restaurants that put soft-boiled eggs in little porcelain holders, and they'd cover it with a knitted thing to keep the egg hot."

"That's the silliest thing I ever heard. I have no desire to see Europe."

Patrick served the eggs and some toast.

"Down there, there in Oklahoma, they've got a toll-free number for the cattle market. I hate having to listen to all this deal on the radio to find what steers brought."

"Steers aren't going to make you anything," Patrick said. He put some English on that.

"Feeding out seven months ain't going to make you anything."

"I never said ranching was any good."

"Talk like that," said his grandfather feistily, "and you won't want to fix nothin."

"Well, just let her fall down then," Patrick said.

"It ain't even historical."

"That's right." Historical? That was a first from the old souse.

"And where would you be running this remuda of yours?"

"On the damn forest service."

"Try it."

"I may."

Patrick's grandfather returned to his eggs, smoldering. Patrick was going to let him make his own tomorrow.

"You ought to back your horses more if you want them to get their butts down," said his grandfather.

"Don't tell me to back my horses. I get their feet under them by making them want to stop."

"They aren't tanks, Patrick."

"I rode some colts you broke twenty years ago. Couldn't turn them around in a twenty-acre pasture."

"Why don't I just cook my own eggs tomorrow? Seems like a little favor spoils your temperament. I remember some of them colts and they turned on a dime. Why, you bugger, I broke Leafy's mother!"

"You cook the eggs."

When he was away Patrick's daydreams fell easily back twenty years to summers riding in the hills, spooking game in the springs and down in the blue, shadowy draws, swimming in the gold dredge, girls present, the cold sky-blue submersion a baptism, the best place for the emerging consciousness of women to grow in suitable containment. Even, suddenly in a West German dance hall, remembering the flood of tears at twelve when he'd killed a spike buck in the same little grove where he and his father always cut their Christmas tree. Before that, hunting coyotes, his grandfather had crawled into a cave near Blacktail and found a ceremonially dressed, mummified Indian warrior on a slab of rock. His grandfather refused to tell anyone where the corpse was, and Patrick wore out two saddle horses looking for it. A friend, Jack Adams, later found it over on Mission Creek. "You do not disturb the Old Ones," his grandfather had said. Then Jack glommed the mummy, making everyone cross. And Patrick himself, on the North Rosebud, had found the scribblings of the phantom ancient Sheepeaters; he had slept in eagle traps and in the coffin-shaped hole in the rock the Crows had made above Massacre Creek. He had seen the skeleton of a Cheyenne girl dressed in an Army coat, disinterred when the railroad bed was widened. Her family had put silver thimbles on every finger to prove to somebody's god that she was a useful girl who could sew. After his father went to work for Boeing and split up with his

mother, Patrick lived with his grandfather and ate so much poached game that the smell of beef nauseated him. He lost the tips of three fingers in his lariat heeling calves in the spring and never went to the movies except to meet girls. He could shoe horses, beat a hunting knife out of an old file, throw a diamond hitch, fix windmills, listen for broken gate valves in the well; and masquerade enough in town to occasionally get his ashes hauled, though he still preferred the sinewy barrel-racers he first met at the gold dredge whose teasing country-ruthless sensuality was somehow smokier than the ten-speeders just learning to roll a number. At sixteen he was jailed twelve times in a row for disorderly conduct; and his father, in the year that he died—a circumstance that left Patrick permanently dented with guilt—borrowed against his share of the ranch and sent Patrick to a preparatory school in the East which thought that a rebellious young cowboy would be a colorful enough addition to a student body that included a Siamese prince with a Corvette, a West German, five Venezuelans and one Negro that they would overlook his poor grades and boisterous history with the law.

They taught him to play soccer. Once again he was in short pants. For a long time he could see his knees in the corners of his eyes when he ran. It made him miss the ball. It was one of the troublesome ways he couldn't escape his own mind. Later, it got worse.

EVIDENTLY SOMEONE PASSING THROUGH GRASSRANGE HAD given Mary a ride as far as Roundup, then dropped her with a social worker there. The conditions that moved this

person to, in effect, turn Mary in were ones that produced concern and not fear: Mary wasn't making sense. The tough district court judge at Roundup had Mary hauled to Warm Springs, which is Montana's state mental institution. She had been detained. But the primary problem was that no one could identify her and Mary wasn't helping. She said that something was always happening to her, but she would tell no one what it was.

Patrick was her custodian once she relinquished her name. He took her home, cruising the interstate in his truck on the intermittently cloudy day. He looked over his sunglasses; he was trying to seem old.

"What'd you read?"

"Two books, over and over."

"What books were they?"

"Books of poetry, Patrick. I read the poems of Saint Theresa of Avila and the poems of Saint John of the Cross. That car has Ohio plates. How many Ohio songs can you name?"

"You make any friends?"

"One trouble with loony bins is you make friends and then you make enemies, and there are these referee-doctors who don't seem to be able to stop this seesaw deal between the two. All they do is keep the patients from savaging each other." She leaned to see herself in the rearview.

"What's the matter with you, anyway?"

"Evidently I can't see life's purpose."

"What do you mean 'evidently'?"

"I mean that that's what they told me. I didn't come up with the idea myself."

"I don't ever think about life's purpose," said Patrick, lying in his teeth.

"Lucky you," she said. "We got enough gas?"

"We do, and there's more where that came from."

Mary was, Patrick thought, such a pretty girl. And she didn't have the neurasthenic glaze that produced what passed for looks among people who would rather raise orchids. Mary had a strong, clear face, a cascade of oaken hair and a lean, athletic figure. But she also had, Patrick thought, a bad attitude. Certainly no bell-jar lady, though.

It made him worry. He was open-minded and interested in other tastes than his own, normally. But, for instance, being Mary's older brother produced, just now, the following question: Who is Saint John of the Cross? I thought Jesus was the one with the cross. It was as if the cross was a party favor, a prize for the most serious face.

"Want to stop at Three Forks and get plastered?" Mary inquired. Her hands made laughing shapes in the air, foretelling gala Three Forks. A saloon conjunction of the Missouri headwaters.

"It isn't the day for that."

"There's another one with Ohio plates."

"I don't care."

"Our home state is being deluged by those of Ohio."

"It's fair."

When the universal shitstorm seemed to mount its darkest clouds, Patrick always said that it was fair. Mary fell silent. Her trouble was she thought it *wasn't* fair. They'd had words about this before. Mary had said his calling everything fair made him more fatal than any Hindu. People like him, she accused, refused smallpox vaccine. Who did he think he was with this fairness? The truth was *nothing* was fair. That's where I've got you, said Patrick.

But Mary's travails had today deprived her of fight. She fixed a stony look upon I-90. She didn't think any of the signs were funny and she stopped counting Ohio plates. Patrick began to worry. He could hear her breathing.

When they spiraled down the Deadrock off-ramp, Mary said, "The other thing is, I'm in a family way." The black-birds shot across the lumberyard, and they both decided that watching them veer between the sawdust stacks was quite the best thing to do.

They passed the smoking waste-burner and log reserves of Big Sky Lumber in silence; and similarly Madison Travertine, where water-cooled saws made weird pink marble slabs out of million-year-old hot-spring mineral accumulations. They crossed Carson's Bridge over the big river while Patrick considered his next question and the mysterious sign painted on the rocks under the high fal-con nests:

PLEASE STOP IT

Nobody knew what the sign meant. In place of direct attention, Patrick accumulated roadside information: ROCK SHOP—AGATES, TERRI'S BEAUTY SHOP, YUMMEE FREEZE, HEREFORDS: MONTANA'S GREATEST TREASURE, U-NAME IT WE'LL FIND IT, a white barn in the turn with a basketball net, a rough-breaks sign, white crosses in Dead Man's Curve, and the broad, good pastures, defined in the earth slits of flood irrigation. A farmer with a shovel watched the passing water.

"Who's the father?"

"Not telling." Drawing a lower eyelid down with her forefinger: Share God's joke on us.

"Okay."

"Do you have any babies in Germany?"

"I don't believe so."

"Little visits you might have made?"

"Who said I made little visits? I was busy in the tank. You need a shower."

"Boy, do I."

"I should warn you, Mary."

"What?"

"*Mother's* visit coming up soon."

"Whew."

"So . . ."

"I don't know. Tough it out, I guess."

"Are you stable?" Patrick inquired.

"Terribly. I wouldn't have given them my name otherwise. I let them circulate my fingerprints while I caught up on some reading." She patted her satchel of books.

Patrick glanced over at Mary, glimpsed the eczema-like condition that left her hands cracked and red from the nervous attacks. They fluttered under his gaze.

"How's Grandpa?" she asked.

"Just a little bit remote. You catch him at the right time and he pours it all out. Otherwise, he's kind of floating around." He was slipping toward Mary.

"That's because he's old," said Mary. "And because he knows he's going to die soon."

Patrick could supply no refutation: He was in midair; he had no family and he wasn't in love. He did try to make his sigh as significant as possible. Mary arched her brows.

"What have you been doing for a living?"

"Let's not go into that," said Mary.

"Where have you been?"

"I was in Belle Fourche, then Denver. I was in Texas for about a month. I was in Grassrange and Moccasin for quite a while, but I *will* not talk about that."

"What'd you think of the Texans?"

"They're like Australians. They're great, actually, as

long as they don't talk about Texas. Can we fix up my
room like it was?"

"It hasn't changed."

"Is the blue reading lamp still there?"

"Yup."

"Bulb work?"

"At last examination."

"Any rules?"

"As a matter of fact, yes," said Patrick. "We do not
allow Negro field chants after three in the morning."

"There's always something," said Mary as they turned
up the road that carried them to the ranch and the hills.
The wild roses shelved green in the bends, and the de-
marcation of light and shadow on the dust seemed artificial. Patrick looked over at Mary. She was staring up the
road toward the ranch and her eyes were not right. He
had certainly made his little joke knowing that she would
not look right when he turned, in the hopes of deflecting
that moment. Patrick didn't know what he saw in her
face—it was pale—but forced to name it, he would have
called it terror. Well, fuck it: Basically the whole thing
was terrifying.

"I could use your help in gentling some of the yearlings," he said, but he got no reply. The air rushed in the
wind vanes.

"Mary, remember the jet that crashed last winter up in
the Absarokas?"

"Yes . . ." She stared at the ranch yard as Patrick glided
toward the turnaround at the barn.

"Well, I found it with my binoculars. I could see a wing
sticking out of the snow, just the tip. It's behind Monitor
Peak. I went up there."

She coddled her satchel. "One book I wouldn't take to a
desert island is a family album."

"Now, what's that supposed to mean?" he asked.

Mary turned and looked full at him. "It means," she said, "that Daddy's not in that plane."

ON SUNDAY, PATRICK WAS INVITED TO THE Z6 FOR LUNCHEON, and for some reason he went. This required a long drive nearly to McRae, where, past the West Stoney River, the Z6 road angled into sweeping foothills. The hills were dry and blue-green with sagebrush, here and there illuminated by small bands of liquid-moving antelope as easy-traveling as sun through windy clouds. The land here seemed the result of an immense and all-eradicating flood, which left rims and ridges as evidence of ancient cresting seas.

The Z6 was what remained of an old English-based land-and-cattle company, the kind that once flourished on the northern grassland, with headquarters in London and Edinburgh; but it had shrunk to the absentee ownership of American cousins, a few of whom contrived to audit its profits and losses from New York City. In July and August the American cousins bought Stetsons and headed west, clogging first-class on a big jet. One cousin, though, Jack Adams, nearing sixty, had been on the ranch most of his life. A good operator, he was a rowdy frequenter of the Montana Club in Helena and a high-speed evader of radar traps. A lot of the people came because of him; but in general they were just day drinkers gathered on a hard green lawn under the inhuman blue sky. Things would grow less intelligent as the day wore on.

Jack came out to meet Patrick as he pulled his truck alongside the cars in a small turnaround facing the lawn and the fine old log buildings, which looked low, solid, somehow refined with their cedar roofs and wood smelling of linseed oil. Patrick admired him because Jack was a cowboy and a gentleman, and so he was pleased that Jack came out carrying him a glass of bourbon, knowing it was Patrick's favorite drink, but knowing also that Patrick, like himself, would drink anything and that, strictly speaking, neither of them drank for fun.

"I hoped you'd come," said Jack. "Anna's made a few gallons of real good Marys, full of nutrition. I thought a little of this with water would help graduate you into nutrition."

"Thank you, sir," said Patrick, slamming the truck door. "To your health."

"Yours. No sense in getting your granddad out today?"

You could see the people, the strangely stylized, bent-at-the-waist postures of people socializing on a lawn.

"All he talks about is the past and the movies. I need to get him back on some middle ground before I can show him. Besides, he doesn't like anybody."

"People go through phases," said Jack. It was not, perforce, banal. "We've all taken a spell or two."

Deke Patwell, the editor of the Deadrock *News*, started toward Patrick. Patwell had left graduate school with little but the habit of dressing in the ill-fitting 1950 seersucker that characterized his professors; but by the time he established himself in Deadrock, he decided that it was the place where the last stand of just folks would take place. This sort of fanciful descent was a kind of religion and had been something of a vice among the privileged

classes for centuries, Marie Antoinette being the most
famous example. Patwell had as little use for Patrick as he
had for the poor and dispossessed. He was a champion of
the average and he meant to make it stick. This attitude
and Patwell's capacity for hard work made the *News* successful. It was a legitimate success.

"How's Patrick?" he said.

"Not bad, Deke."

"Enjoying the gathering?" Deke was always rakish
when he managed to leave his wife at home.

"Oh, yeah."

"Anything newsworthy up your way?"

"No, it's been awful quiet."

"We thought it best to ignore Mary's little run-ins."

Patrick felt his blood rising. "Like what?"

"Well, you've been away. And like I say, we didn't see
fit to print." Little homecoming presents. Lawn war.

"I appreciate it," said Patrick as best he could, wondering why Patwell was establishing this debt. Maybe just
the husbandry of someone who daily had to call in the
repayment of small favors.

"Time for my refill," said Patwell. "And call me if you
get anything up your way."

Patrick walked toward the lawn. The lawn was Anna's
idea. Anna was Jack's wife. Anna did not belong to the
dude-ranch-wife set with the shaved back of the neck and
boot-cut Levis; there were certain perquisites for having
raised children and done well that she regarded as indis-
pensable. One was a lawn; others were New York clothes,
a restaurant-size gas stove, a Missouri fox-trotter horse
and a German Olympic-grade .22 rifle to shoot gophers
with. The first time a luncheon guest shoved a Ferragamo
pump into a gopher colony, Anna ordered the rifle. In
early summer she sat upstairs beneath the steeply angled

roof in her bathrobe, moving the crosshairs over the rolled green expanse, looking for rodents in the optics. Jack learned to use the back door as he came and went to the pens and barn, the report of the small-caliber rifle becoming, year by year, less audible.

The Bloody Marys were in a huge cut-glass bowl, which rested in a cattle-watering tank filled with ice. No one had fanned out far from this place and Patrick got a quick survey: a few people he already knew, Anna, who just winked, and a handsome young couple he'd never seen. The husband wore a good summer jacket and a pair of boots the height of his knee, outside his pants. An oilman, Patrick thought. Oilmen, whatever else they might wear, needed one outstanding sartorial detail to show that their oil was on ranches. And by God, if there was enough oil, they'd go ahead and put cows on those ranches and wear their boots like that. You wanted to be sure no one thought you were a damn parts salesman.

Patrick still had his bourbon and had planned a slow approach, but Anna swept him in, introducing him with the "Captain" prefix. Deke Patwell was deftly escorting an inheritrix from Seattle named Penny Asperson and interviewing an orthodontist–land speculator from Missoula via Cleveland named, believe it or not, something-or-other Lawless. All Patrick could remember was that last name. And there was the couple, sure enough oil: Claire Burnett and her husband, whose real name was John but who was already, in his thirties, called Tio, which is Mexican for uncle and is a rather flattering nickname for one who aspires to be a *patrón*. But Tio was vivid anyway, pierceybright, oilman feisty, and his wife was a knockout. Patrick knew their name, a little bit, because of horses.

The conversation was lively already. A boy had been shot and killed on a ranch recently for trespassing. Claire and Tio looked baffled at this bit of local color. Deke Patwell slid comfortably into his local-expert mode and sternly explained that only the ranchers' reputation for being trigger-happy kept them safe and their way of life intact. Then playfully he tugged at her sleeve and said, "Claire, you do horses so well. Let me and Tio do current events. Later you do house. Anything else is just five-o'clock news."

"Where is the dead boy's family?" Claire asked. Tio then scooped down into Bloody Marys. Deke caught his glance and they walked over under the cottonwoods. Claire turned to Patrick. Tio had bought Deke's views.

"I'm not going to ask you what you think."

"Yes, ma'am."

"People side up with Tio because they want his business."

"I don't want his business."

"What are you captain of?"

"Tanks."

"See, they know how shocking their thinking is. They just want it to set them apart. Has nothing to do with that boy— Tanks?"

Patrick tried to decide whether good country living, money, self-esteem or the kind of routine maintenance that begins with pumice-stoning the callouses of one's feet and ends somewhere between moisture packs and myopic attention to individual split ends produced Claire's rather beautiful physical effect. Claire said she didn't know who meant what anymore. Baseball players had Daffy Duck haircuts sticking out from under their billed caps, rock 'n' roll stars all wore sateen warm-up jackets like the baseball players', and the President was passing out in a foot race while Russians installed nerve gas around ballistic-missile silos. So who could tell whether or not that little old editor was copping an attitude or whether Tio was just kicking back into his good-buddy act because he was in someone else's state?

Patrick said, "I don't know."

She said, "What do you mean 'I don't know'?"

"I don't know and I don't care."

"Let's go to the house and refill your bourbon. I can see you casting a funny eye at those mixed drinks. Did you train a mare named Leafy?"

They started toward the house.

"Yes, I did."

"What do you want for her?"

"Well, she's just my horse."

"I saw her at Odessa."

"She was there."

"Did you ever breed her?"

"No."

They walked into the cool wood-chambered living room with the buffalo rugs and the Indian blankets and the peyote boxes and the beaded parfleches on the deeply oiled logs.

"*Would* you ever breed her?"

"If she let me know she wanted to have a baby."

"You ought to breed to our stud. I presume she's cycling."

Patrick just didn't reply. He looked up from his freshly drawn glass of sour mash, a smile on his face that crossed all the silence of immediate conversational aftermath.

He took a long, kindly look at this young woman, thought of their banter, saw in her confidence that she enjoyed it, too, the way grade-schoolers like to slug each other out of sheer attraction. Then he wondered if he would find Tio less estimable the next time he saw him, which would be in a few moments, or if he would gather that Claire was just in a world of her own, set out upon one of the ineluctable trajectories of conflict that can be blamed upon something long ago, a book, a parent, an aging nun, a baton dropped in front of a sold-out stadium. I don't know, he thought, and I don't care. Yes, I care, but I won't.

"Ever hear the joke about the escaped circus lion down in Texas? He nearly starved to death. Every time he growled at one of those Texans, it scared the shit out of him. And when he jumped on him, it knocked all the hot air out. So there was nothing left to eat."

She said, "I'm from Oklahoma. My God, is that a joke?"

"Let's go inside. I could interpret the wall hangings. They're Northern Cheyenne."

"Thanks," she smiled, "but we done had Comanche down at home." She dropped her chin and examined him.

He thought he could see perhaps the tiniest acquiescence, though not quite anything he could hold her to. He found her engaging and probably as strong as he was, that is to say, not particularly strong or, rather, strong in the wrong ways.

"We're more fun than the luncheon guests," said Claire bravely as she went into the hard glare over the lawn, gone in her bounding step toward the people at the tank. It could be said that Patrick's mild stalling, giving Claire a lead, came from a very slight sly motive in him, one that he recognized and resolved to give a bit of thought to. The stalling left him among the mops in the front hall, hooks holding worn-out hats, irrigating boots, a pair of old dropshank spurs and a twelve-gauge: a basic tool kit.

Then when Patrick stepped onto the lawn, Tio was walking resolutely toward him, long-strided in his tall calfskin boots. What's this? Well, for one thing, thought

Patrick, it's the first time I've seen eighteen-karat-gold oil-derrick blazer buttons.

"Patrick."

"Tio."

"They say you're a horseman."

"Something of one," said Patrick, thinking, Your wife was too friendly. He was a little ahead of himself.

"Do you like good cow ponies?"

"Yes." Were there people who didn't?

Tio plunged his hands in his pockets, then leaned the full weight on his straightened arms, tilted slightly forward from the waist, weight in the pockets. Tell you what I'm gonna do. One knee moving rapidly inside its pant leg. "Claire say I got a stud?"

"Yes, she did."

"Tell you much about the old pony?"

"No—"

"Say he was good?"

"She thought I ought to breed this cutting mare of mine to him."

"Well, you should, old buddy. This pony'll cut a cow, now. I mean the whole bottom drops out and he's lookin *up* at them cattle. He traps his cattle and just showers on them."

"Well, I'm gonna ride this mare another couple years yet. She's my number-one deal."

"*Plus*, this pony comes right from the front of the book. Peppy San out of an own daughter of Gunsmoke. It idn't any way he can get out of traffic fast enough to keep hisself from being a champion."

Patrick wasn't much interested. He said, "Well, when I get something to breed, I'll take a hard look at him."

"I want you to breed that old Leafy mare. This stud of

mine is young and he needs mares like that to put them good kind of babies on that ground. You know how long Secretariat's cannon bone is?"

"Sure don't."

"Nine inches. So's this colt's. That's what makes an athlete. That'n a good mind. This colt's got one of them, too. His name is American Express, but I call him Cunt because that's all he has on his mind. He's a stud horse, old Cunt is. But I'm like that. You were always lookin for a smoke, I'd call you Smoke."

"What d'you call Claire?"

"Claire sixty percent of the time, and Shit when she don't get it correct, which is right at forty."

Patrick thought, I wonder if they'll ever teach him English. Maybe he doesn't want to learn. Maybe you can't be an old buddy and speak English. Patrick would rather hear a cat climbing a blackboard. And he didn't like what Tio called his wife forty percent of the time. In fact, he just didn't like Southwesterners. It wasn't even cow country to Patrick. It was yearling country. There were no cowboys down there significantly. There were yearling boys and people who fixed windmills. After that, you put in dry wall on the fourteenth story of a condo in Midland, where some cattleman did it all on a piece of paper with a solid-gold ball-point pen and a WATS line: a downtown rancher, calling everything big he had little and old, and calling his wife shit; the first part of the West with gangrene. Dance the Cotton-Eyed Joe and sell it to the movies.

Here came Jack Adams with another bourbon; probably spotted that look in Patrick's eye and sought to throw fat on the fire. People often have this kind of fun with problem drinkers. But Patrick was determined to be somebody's angel, and they wouldn't catch him out today. Instead he started back to the company, excusing himself. Made a nice glide of it.

Deke Patwell and Penny Asperson were passing a pair of binoculars back and forth, trying to find the property lines a thousand yards uphill. "Not strong enough," said Deke, putting the glasses away. "We'd have to walk up there, and we know how we feel about that." His mouth made a sharp downward curve.

Anna said, "We use the National Forest anyway. So I don't know what that property line's supposed to mean." She gave the Bloody Marys a thoughtful stir.

"You will when the niggers start backpacking," said Deke Patwell. "Oh God, that's me being ironic."

"Anna's the lucky type," Patrick said. "She'll get O. J. Simpson and an American Express card."

Claire said, "You sprinkle this much?"

"After July," Anna said. "It's a luxury but we've got a good well. If it was Jack, we'd be waist-deep in sage and camass and just general prairie, and the ticks would be walking over us looking for a good home."

The buildings, which made something of a compound of the lawn, moved their long shadows, lengthening toward the blue sublight of the spruce trees; but the real advent of midafternoon was signaled when Deke Patwell passed out. Everyone gathered around him as his tall form lay crumpled in his oddly collegiate lawn-party clothes. He was only out for a moment, which was too bad, because he had grown strident with his drunkenness, especially as to his social theories. He had been drawing a bright picture of Jew-boy legions storming the capitol at Helena when his eyes went off at an angle and he buckled.

Then he was trying to get up. He rolled mute, imploring eyes at the people surrounding him, threw up and inhaled half of it. It was like watching him drown. Jack bent over, stuck a hand in his mouth and said, "I'd say the Hebrews got the capitol dome."

Anna said to Jack firmly, "Go inside and warsh your hands." Deke let go another volley and said he didn't feel so good.

Minor retribution crept into Patrick's mind. He said, "Maybe a drink would perk you up." Deke cast a vengeful glance up to him, said he would remember that, then tipped over onto one shoulder on the lawn and gave up. His plaid summer jacket was rolled around his shoulder blades, and a slab of prematurely marbled flesh stood out over his tooled belt.

Patrick ambled toward the little creek that bordered one side of the lawn. Perfect wild chokecherries made a topiary line against the running water, which held small wild trout, long used to the lawn parties. But then Penny Asperson followed him, and when he looked back, he caught Claire's observation of the pursuit. In his irritation he thought Penny was thundering toward him. There were yellow grosbeaks crawling on the chokecherry branches, more like little mammals than birds.

"Bloody Deke," said Penny. "If he'd had the gumption, we'd be up at the boundary. He'd be sober and the air would be full of smoldering glances." Penny's broad sides heaved with laughter. "*Now* look. And he smells." Patrick wished to speak to her of carbohydrates and chewing each bite twenty-seven times. But she was, after all, a jolly girl.

"The smell's the worst of it," Patrick said agreeably. "I thought Jack was courageous to free his tongue."

"It takes a man to do that."

"And Jack is a man," said Patrick, a little tired of the

silliness. A pale-blue moth caught one wing on the water and a cutthroat trout arose beneath it, drifted downstream a few feet, sucked it in and left a spiraling ring to mark the end of the moth.

"Did you forget your rod?" Penny winked.

"Oh, what a naughty girl."

"Patrick."

"Penny. Let's go back."

"I think we should," said Penny Asperson. "Or we'll start talk." They walked back to the tank, Patrick doing all he could to control his gait, to keep from breaking into a little jog. Tio was talking firmly with Claire, knocking her lightly in the wishbone with his drink hand, for emphasis.

As Patrick passed, Tio said, "Wait a sec, Captain. This goes for you." Patrick joined them, trying to see just as much of Claire as he could with his peripheral vision. He wanted to put his hand on her skin. Tio went on in a vacuum.

"I need to have this little old stallion in motion," Tio said. "I travel too much to keep him galloped, and besides, I don't like to ride a stud. Cousin Adams tells me you can make a nice bridle horse, and if you can get this horse handling like he ought to, that'd be better than me having to mess with him every time I get off the airplane. You're in the horse business, aren't you?"

"Sure am," said Patrick. Claire shifted her weight a little. "Can I change his nickname?" Claire reddened.

"You can call him Fido's Ass for all I care. Just get that handle on him. I'm going in to look at old Jack's artifacts. Supposed to have a complete Indian mummy he found in the cliffs." He strode toward the house in his tall calfskin boots. "We gone try and give that mummy a name."

Anna appeared in the door.

"Patrick!" she called. "You've got to take Deke home. He's spoiled a storm-pattern Navajo and now he's just got to go home."

"Coming!" called Patrick, and Claire was halfway to the house—in effect, fleeing.

Patrick undertook the loading of Deke Patwell. Anna apologized for making Patrick accept this onerous detail, adding that otherwise it would have to be Jack and it was sort of Jack's party. They locked Deke's door where he slumped, and turned the wind vane in his face. His lip slid against the glass.

For the first couple of miles toward town, Deke tried slinging himself upright in a way that suggested he was about to make a speech. He slumped back and watched the hills fly by while the hard wind raveled his thin auburn hair.

"I didn't like your comment, buddy."

"What comment?" Patrick asked.

" 'Have another drink, perk you up.' I don't like getting a raft of shit like that just because I want to cut loose on the weekend." When he tried to spit through the wind vane, it came back in on him.

"I probably shouldn't have said it. It was a joke."

"It wasn't funny." They passed the corrals, scales and loading chutes of the local livestock association. There were a couple of horses and an Australian shepherd in one section, waiting for their owners to come and do something with them. Patrick let a little silence fall.

"You come home," Deke went on, "just pick up where you left off. Goddamned officer."

"Well, I wasn't much of an officer."

Patrick was mostly successful in shutting Deke out of his mind, like listening to the same day's news on the radio for the second time. They were driving along the switching yards, and probably because of Deke, he began to think of the old rummies who used to be such a part of a big yard like this. Electric engines, good security lights and cross-referenced welfare lists stole our bums, thought Patrick. When the American West dried up once and for all, those migrant birds, the saints of cheap Tokay, began to look bad to the downtown merchants, to the kayakers and trout fishermen, even to the longhairs with tepee poles on the tops of their Volkswagens, who thought the rummies were like the white men who had corrupted the Indians with whiskey in Bernard De Voto's *Across the Wide Missouri*. Anyway, they were gone.

Deke was still maneuvering for an insult; but they were nearly to his house now on Gallatin Street. Deke knew his time was running out, and Patrick was hurrying a little because he had begun to find himself paying a bit of attention, starting with a slurred polemic against his grandfather, which didn't work because it listed things about the old man Patrick liked. They pulled in front of the brick house as Deke started in on Patrick's sister again. And for the first time Patrick thought, This is going to be close. Deke Patwell must have thought so too, because he opened his door before announcing the following: "She's *immoral*. And I have every reason to *believe* she uses drugs." It was quite a delivery.

Patrick kicked him through the open door onto the sidewalk. Deke's head snapped down on the concrete but recovered, leaving him on all fours, blood in the corner of his mouth and vomit on his period costume. He kept printing the blood on the palm of his hand to be sure he'd been injured. Mrs. Patwell appeared in the door. The tableau was a basic stacked deck illustrating Patrick's penchant for violence. "You'll live to regret this," she said with a compression between her eyes. Two children appeared on the sidewalk, and one of them, unable to make much of these grownups, could think of nothing more salutory than to sail his frisbee over the recumbent form of Deke, yelling, "Catch it, Mr. Patwell! Catch it!" It seemed appropriate to Mrs. Patwell to go after the kids, who scattered into the wilderness of back lots and yard fences. She didn't have their speed, their quickness. Patrick headed home. He felt quite giddy.

9

PATRICK WOUND ALONG TO THE EAST OF THE RIVER. IT BURST out blue in segments whenever a hay or grain field dropped away. Also, there were tall mountains and a blue sky. But they only go so far. Patrick would have liked a silent, reverent involving of himself with Claire. In another era he could have been her coachman. "Might I assist, Ma'moiselle?" She can't help but notice how good he is with the horses. One must put aside one's silk-bound missal and duck off into this grove of elms. The horses graze; the springs of the little coach can be heard for miles. Screeching like fruit bats.

Patrick approached the ranch as though in an aircraft, sitting well back, making small adjustments of the wheel with outstretched arms as the buildings loomed, moving his head with a level rotary motion. We are making our approach. The stewardesses are seated in the little fold-down chairs. Claire is alone in first class; the surface of her gin and tonic tilts precisely with each directional adjustment. And now we are stopped and the dogs are gathering. Lilacs are reflected in the windows. Grandpa

dashes to the truck. Must be with the ground crew, perhaps a baggage handler. That or a fucking woodpecker.
Turn off the ignition. Engine diesels and quits. Opposite
door flung open by Crew Chief Grandpa. This man is
excited.

"*Your sister has gone mad!*"

"What are you talking about?"

"I smelt turpentine," the old man roared. "I went down
to her room and she was painting everything. She was
painting curtains! I couldn't get her to listen to me. She
just talked on like I wasn't there." Patrick's heart sank.
"When I went back, she was gone."

"Where is she now?"

"That's it. I don't know!"

They were hurrying toward the house.

"Why are we walking this way, then?"

"Well, maybe she's back in her room. Pat, what the
hell's the matter with her?"

"I really don't know." He didn't, either.

They hurried up the walkway and went in through the
kitchen. Patrick could smell the paint and turpentine from
here; and as he went down the hallway, it got more intense. He expected for some reason that she would be in
her room, and his grandfather, pressing behind him,
seemed to agree. Patrick knocked and got no answer. So
he opened the door. She wasn't there. If it wasn't for the
fact that the paint was blue, the room would have looked
like the scene of a massacre. A house-painter's broad
brush soaked blue paint into the bedclothes. The upended
gallon can directed a slowly moving blue tongue under
the dresser. There was no turpentine in sight. The curtains had begun to dry stickily, with a cheap surrealistic
effect, around a window full of sky and clouds.

They went back to the kitchen. But by that time the

barn was already burning. It was visible from the kitchen, a steady horizontal pall moving downwind from between the logs. Patrick started for the doors. "Call the Fire Department! I'll run to the barn."

Patrick sprinted around the bunkhouse to the barn. He climbed the wooden strakes into the haymow. Mary sat under the rafters. The hay was on fire and the wind blew through the separations in the logs, creating innumerable red fingers of fire that worked through the bales, collided and leaped up into longer-burning lines, a secretive, vascular fire.

"We are without tents. We'll do anything to stay warm. There are tracks in the drifts. We used to have a chairlift to get us down, but my mother interfered with the mechanism and confiscated my lift pass. She put rats in the last empty gondola."

"I'll get you down," said Patrick. "But we must go now. And stop talking like that."

"Yes," said Mary. "We must think of the baby."

The volunteers arrived in a stocky yellow truck, threw the intake hose into the creek and doused the barn inside and out. Steam roared into the sky and cast shadows over the house like storm-driven clouds. The firemen were dressed in yellow slickers and had plexiglass shields in front of their faces. They guided the heavy canvas-covered hose inside their elbows and against their backs, like loafers leaning on a village fence. Only one man aimed the nozzle into the smoke and flames. Patrick thought that he could see in their expressions that this was an unnecessary fire. Perhaps it was his imagination.

Afterward the phone rang; it was Deke Patwell, still somewhat blurred. The phone in Patrick's hand felt like a blunt instrument.

"Understand you've had a barn fire."

"That's right, Deke."

"Any suspicion of foul play or is it all in the family?"

"It's all in the family," said Patrick.

"Hope like heck it stays out of the papers."

"Thank you, Deke. I'm one hundred percent certain that it will. You know what I mean, Deke? I'm really that sure."

It did seem, though, that Deke was intoning some small, minatory announcement and that it might have been better if Patrick hadn't kicked him onto the sidewalk. But weren't there a few things one was obliged to do? Perhaps he hadn't paid enough attention to Mary over the years. He might have written more often. If he had, Patrick considered, the kick might have been vague or symbolic and not shooting some ass-pounding moron onto the sidewalk. And Mrs. Patwell pursuing the children like a wounded pelican—that, too, would have its consequences. The Patwells had the solidest marriage in Deadrock.

❖ **10** ❖

PATRICK STOOD AT THE COUNTER AT FARM NEEDS AND bought ten iodized-salt blocks, five hundred pounds of whole oats and a thin twenty-eight-foot lariat. Standing at the counter, he could stare across the street to the grain elevator, the railroad tracks; and coming out of the east, he saw the Burnetts' car; and when it passed, he saw Claire at the wheel. He followed the car with his eyes and without moving his head.

"Let me just take my slip," he said to the salesman. "I'll swing through for the oats in a bit."

He followed the car discreetly, thinking, She doesn't know this truck anyway, left at Main, up a few blocks until she stopped. He parked in front of J. C. Penney's; he saw her get out of her car and walk into the MyWay Cafe. Patrick slapped his pockets for change. The meter maid was two cars away. He had no coins and here she came.

"I'm afraid I'm out of change."

"I'll give you time," she said.

"That's all right."

"My gosh, it'll save you five dollars." Her grab on the facts was evaporating. The meter itself seemed like a joke.

"Write me up," said Patrick, jauntily heading across the street, the meter maid staring at him with her pad of tickets. She began to write. She wrote hard and she wrote mean.

Patrick sauntered along the MyWay front window; but then when he gave his eyes one cut to the interior, he found himself locked in gaze with Claire. He waved, then mimed may-I-join-you? As though talking to a lip reader. She just *smiled.* In we go, thought Patrick; my back is to the meter.

The MyWay is sandwiched between the Wagon Wheel western store and Good Looks, ladies' fashions. It's kind of a shotgun arrangement, white inside with orange tables. It has a clock that reads twelve o'clock, three o'clock, 7-Up and nine o'clock. It has a reversible sign hanging in the door that says, OPEN, but from the customers' view reads, SORRY, WE'RE CLOSED. It has candy in a display called Brach's Candyland. It has a Safety and Protection on the Job poster, a dispenser for black hair-combs guaranteed for ten years and still only thirty cents. A huge box of S.O.S. says it will cut grease quicker. It's an A.F. of L. union house and smoking is permitted. It seemed ready for a nuclear attack.

Patrick stood next to the waitress while she finished telling Claire something. Claire cut her eyes over to him, smiled, then paid polite attention to the waitress.

"My brother can lie his way out of anything," she was saying, "but not *me*. I ain't sayin I wasn't in the wrong. My pickup was flat movin, comin around that old canyon. I'll tell *you*. But this smoky says, 'You wanta pull it over or drive fifty-five?' I shoulda outrun his ass. Okey-doke, let me get this. How bout you?"

"Black coffee," said Patrick, and sat down.

"How're you-all?" Claire had eyes that shone.

"Never better."

"Bite?"

"No thanks. I came to town for grain."

"I was hoping you were following me."

"I'll follow you next time I see you." To the waitress: "Coffee is all."

"Where can you get something to eat in Deadrock?"

"You're eating now."

"How can you tell?"

"You can feel it in your throat."

She chewed slowly and watched Patrick a moment before speaking again. He started to get jumpy.

"May I share my impressions with you about Montana?"

"Oh, but you can," said Patrick in a tinny voice.

"An area of high transience. But while folks are here, they are proud of it. I have seen no marches to the state flag yet, but I have noticed your extremely direct state motto: '*Oro y Plata.*' I know that stands for gold and silver. It shows a real go-getter attitude."

"Is that good, Claire?"

"Back where I come from, your shoe salesman strikes oil in the side lot and starts a ranch with headquarters in the Cayman Islands, then he buys a show horse, the bull that wins the Houston Fat Stock Show and a disco."

"Whoever did that?"

"My father! I'm *nouveau riche*! We're just not old family. The foundation for old families in Oklahoma is early-day stealing, before the advent of good records."

Patrick changed his mind and ordered pumpkin pie. He could see upper torsos passing the front window. He could see newspaper readers at other tables, revealing only their hands, which seized either end of the newsprint and stretched it to their eyes.

"What got you to come to Montana?" Patrick was growing tired of hearing himself ask these sap questions. Still, he couldn't break out of it. I'm no sap, he thought.

"Tio sold the cabin cruiser. We had it in Corpus. It was to go to Padre Island. Padre Island is kind of a redneck Riviera. It has great birds. But Tio kept running aground. Tio has kind of a health problem. So when the Coast Guard said they wouldn't rescue us anymore, Tio said, 'That does it. I'll spend my money in another area. The northern grasslands, for instance.'"

"Has it been a good move?"

"The jury is still out. Tio's starved for conversation. Nobody does much oil here, not to mention cattle futures, row crops or running horses."

"Did Tio inherit his money?" I've had enough of Tio. Why am I asking this?

"Let's say he got it somehow. But he's done right smart with what he got." It was a hollow advertisement.

"I see."

"And in some ways he's a very private person. About the only way somebody'd get his telephone number at home is if one of his bird dogs run away and they got it off its collar."

Patrick moved upon the pie, ate half of it, swigged

some coffee and asked (this will get her off balance), "When was the last time you blushed?" He blushed. Sapland.

"At my wedding." It didn't get her off balance.

"Really."

"Oklahoma girls are trained to pull off one of those in their lives. After that, they are never required to do it again."

"I blushed at my First Communion."

"Are you a Catholic?"

"I consider myself one."

"You mean you aren't practicing."

"That is correct."

"Then why do you consider yourself one?"

"It makes me feel I'm just that much less of a white man."

"Aha!"

Patrick managed to pay for the ice cream and walk Claire to her car. He held the door for her. She ducked in and, talking to him, made a blind reach for the climate control, then the sound system. Four speakers boom in Jamaican: *"Natty don't work for no CIA."* She grinned.

"Amo shuffle on home," she said. "Babylon by Cadillac."

"Can you give me a lift to my truck?"

"Get on in."

The cool interior was wonderful, the simulated-walnut dashboard reassuring in that someone cared to keep up appearances. No high tech here, just plastic that ached for ancient hardwoods.

"Take your first right." They cruised up Main and turned. "Sure is nice and cool in here."

"I don't imagine that's much of a problem in Montana. What in the world do people do in the winter?"

"Just hang around the salad bars. There's nothing quite like Green Goddess at thirty below. Take another right."

Two more rights and they were back where they started, in front of Patrick's truck. Patrick opened the door. "Thanks a lot."

"Sure enjoyed circling the block with you. And say, the conversation was great."

"Same to you goes double."

Claire smiled. "I like dragging Main in the heat of the day. Been crazy about it since I don't know when."

"Good-bye."

"Good-bye."

Patrick thought, This is more horrible than a glint of bayonets in the concertina wire.

❖ 11 ❖

THE NEXT DAY, PATRICK THOUGHT THAT A GOOD MEAL MIGHT help Mary. His grandfather was bitching about the cuisine as well. So he drove to town for some supplies. He thought first about tea-smoked duck but remembered that all the ducks left in the freezer were green-winged teal— too small, really, for what he wanted. He recalled the advice of the master chef Paul Bocuse: Shop first, then decide what you're going to make; attend to the seasons— no strawberries for Christmas dinner, no game for Easter.

He entered the IGA store already primed, then excited once he had the shopping cart. He found black mushrooms, cloud ears and Szechwan peppers without a hitch. He was on a run. He found a fifty-pound bag of beautiful long-grain South Carolina rice effortlessly. The hugecloved California garlics and fresh ginger set him on his heels; so that when he found the strong, perfect leeks bound together with paper-wrapped wire, smelled the earth in the darkened roots and felt their cool bulk against his hands, he knew the enemy had been driven from his fortification. Three fat chickens, small projectilelike cucumbers, fresh spinach to make streamers to mark the depth of his clear pork soup, a case of Great Falls Select from the cooler and yes, a bit of help to the truck would be nice. Put the leeks up front with me. I'm a captain, good-bye.

The grandfather and Mary sat at the round kitchen table while Patrick worked. He boned and skinned the chicken, then sliced it all into uniform strips. He had first cooked on the lid of an old Maytag washing machine—a basic utensil in the mountains. But now he had a south San Francisco hard-steel wok, restaurant-sized.

"What in hell you been doing to support yourself?" Grandfather asked Mary.

"I worked for a veterinarian."

"What happened?"

"I lost the job."

"For what?"

"I was fired for taking animal tranquilizers."

"You *what?*"

Patrick made a rectilinear pile of the chicken slivers. He mashed the garlic with his cleaver, removed the pale-varnish papery skins, then minced the peppers; the same with the ginger—both arrayed alongside the chicken. He broke up the serrano peppers and spilled the rattling minute seeds into the sink.

"What else have you been doing, Mary?" asked Grandfather in a yelp. Granddad under stress always grew doglike.

"Well, let's see. Got pregnant and, uh, went to Warm Springs. You know, *the big nut house.*"

"Oh, well, great, Mary."

Using the cleaver, Patrick split the well-washed leeks into cool white-and-green lengths, dividing them on the steel. He could feel the animosity through his back.

"I hear you've gone into the movies, Grandpa."

"I was just having a look around. Anyway, nobody knows where that damned movie went to. I certainly don't, but I'm darned mad about it."

Patrick fired up the wok, the cooking shovel resting inside. He poured in the oil. In a moment numerous small bubbles migrated vertically through it.

"Then I joined up with some communists from Canada."

Patrick turned from the stove. "Can it," he said to Mary. "And *you*, shut up about the movies."

He dropped the garlic in, then the ginger, then the Szechwan peppers, then the serranos. They roared in the oil and cooked down gorgeously. Arrayed around the wok were leeks, chicken, yellow crookneck squash, soy sauce, rice wine, salt—everything *jingbao*, explosion-fried. He raced about setting the table, put the wok next to a six-pack and served with the cooking shovel.

"Do I have to use chopsticks?" the grandfather wailed.

"You better if you're going to China."

"I'll bring my own utensils. Say, who said I'm going to China?"

"Use the chopsticks, Gramp. They won't let you take silverware through the metal detector at the airport. Y'know, because of international terrorism."

"Tomorrow can we have chili?"

"No, you're having a can of tuna and your own can opener, you goddamned sonofabitch."

"I like water-packed tuna, but no oil for me, please."

"Eat what I made you."

Mary stared into her plate, held each piece up as though trying to see through it, then returned it to her plate. She went to the kitchen for a glass of water and was gone a little too long. Patrick returned to his own meal: She ought to be darling when she gets back.

"Used to be a real stockman's country," said his grandfather, eating quite rapidly once he forgot the chili and tuna fish. "No one retained mineral rights in a ranch trade. No farm machinery." Mary came back. "Strange people here and there. One man with a saddled horse tied under his bedroom window at all times. Southern man with his boys chained up at night. Irrigator from Norway hiding in a car body from the hailstones. Me and old what's-his-name buying hootch out back at the dances. Pretty schoolteacher used to ski to them dances, packing her gown. This Virginian used to do the nicest kind of log-work'd get tanked up and fight with a knife. Old Warren Butterfield killed him and buried him past the Devil's Slide, only not too many people known that at that time and Warren's at the rest home, fairly harmless I'd say. Virginian needed it, anyhow. I could show you the spot. Shot him with a deer rifle. Virginian couldn't remember pulling the knife out on Warren at the dance. Warren told me that couple days later and he went up to shoot him, that Virginian couldn't figure for the life of him why. It gave Warren second thoughts, but he let him have it. Everybody was pleased, big old violent cracker with protruding ears, ruining the dances. Nicest kind of logwork, though, used a froe, chopped at them timbers between his feet, looked like they'd been through the planer down to the mill. After that, everybody went to frame. No more Virginian."

Mary said, "Kill, shoot, whack, stab, chop."

"Well, that's how it was."

Mary looked up past Patrick and said, "Who are you?" Patrick stared at her an instant and turned. It was Tio, standing in the doorway. He suspended his Stetson straw horizontal to his stomach.

"Knocked, guess nobody heard me. I see you, Pat?"

"Surely," said Patrick, getting up and leaving his napkin and following Tio outside.

"I'll be listening to murder stories," Mary said. Tio looked back, made a grimacing, uncomprehending smile, which she received blankly. "How y'all?" Tio tried.

"Say, thanks for dinner," bayed the grandfather. "And don't forget: Water-packed, or *n-o* spells no!"

Outside, Tio asked, "You cook, Pat?"

"Yeah, sure do. I like it a lot."

"Make chili?"

"Yup. My grandfather just requested it."

"Like a tejano or this northern stew-type deal?"

"Tejano."

"I make Pedernales chili à la L.B.J. Crazy bout L.B.J. Eat that chili in homage, old buddy. Y'all through eatin, weren't you?"

"We were, actually."

"What'n the hell was that?"

"Chinese food."

"Old boys have got more oil than anybody thinks."

"Who's this?"

"Chinese. We sit here?"

"Sure, this'd be fine." They sat on the wood rack where water had once sluiced to cool milkcans not that long ago, before the supermarket. Patrick could see the big anthracite Cadillac nosed up to the straw stack.

"It's a hell of a picturesque deal out here," said Tio, looking all around. "Has to be an escape. About a month of this, though, I'd start missing my wells and my travel agent, in that order. Getting to where I can't hardly stand a vacation. The same time I'm looking to farm everything out. Supposed to be delegating. But delegating for what? Got everything a guy'd ever need. We knocked off work and redid an old sugar refinery down in the islands, then moved to Saint-Barts. Every time we went down to dinner, we'd be lined up behind these Kuwait sand niggers waving three different currencies at the waiter. Me, I took the old lady and went back to Tulsa, got her a little hidey-hole and a bunch of charge accounts, and threw her to fortune. I'm not saying I farmed *that* out. But I figured this: If nature's going to run its course, an intelligent man best stand back from his television set. Well, nothing happened. By the time I got a hundred million in help on a little offshore daydream of mine, she'd bought maybe two dresses and was back breaking colts like somebody supposed to call you sir. Still now, Pat, my conscience is a-nagging at me all the while. Hell, look at you. 'What's the point of all this falderal,' ole Pat is asking hisself."

"You read my mind." Patrick thought, I must have a stupid, vacant face for people to run on at me like this. I must have big jug-handle ears.

"Well, the point is, good buddy, I took my chances. And there wasn't any chances. Old Shit is bulletproof. You could drop her anywhere and she'd land on her feet. *Plunk*. She could run a ranch while Tio saw to his oil and radio stations and stayed out on that road to where *his* nature could take its little course. If you had enough Catholic churches up in this country, I could put her on a few sections with half a dozen top kind of wetbacks. They're like Brahman cattle—it takes quite a little to hold them, and it's them churches that'll do it. And really, a guy'd rather leave his wife with them than white trash.

See, a Mexican will know where he idn't posed to mess, where your white trash might have him some delusions of grandeur. Some of them been President."

"Are you telling me she's not going back to Tulsa with you?" Patrick needed a translator.

"I'm just saying I'm gonna be traveling all summer. Look, we don't have children. We can't have them. At first, I took it like a man. I said it's all my fault. I've got an undiagnosed situation with my nerves that could be passed on. I was set to send her to California to one of these Nobel prize–winner sperm banks. Then we found it was her. Some kind of lady's plumbing problem that's to where you can't just go on in and fix it. Then my doctor at home told me the nerves was nothing to worry about. It was iron-poor, tired blood."

"I don't quite see what this has to—"

"Lookit here. I'm not saying Tio's going to do no replacing. But here's this fortune settin in Tulsa getting bigger daily. Where's Tio's son and heir? How's this dynasty supposed to happen? Well, maybe it doesn't happen. But a realistic Tio is a Tio who keeps his buns in circulation in case something magic comes out of the woodwork; and you can't be haulin your old lady on trips like that. She don't haul good to start with."

Patrick thought hard to understand why this warranted calling him away from dinner. "Did you want me to help out in some way?"

"Truthfully, she's gonna have to have someone around. You've both got interests in common with these fool nags. Plus I'll back every horse prospect y'all might unearth. But I just want you to be kind of a big brother to the little gal. Old Jack Adams tells me you're solider than a pre-Roosevelt dollar and you'd be the guy, especially if you watched your drinking. She's gonna need company and it's almost never gonna be me."

"How in the world could you ever arrange a thing like that?" Patrick used the word "arrange" on purpose.

"I just did! Trust Tio's fine Italian hand. Movin people from one place to another has always been my best lick."

Patrick hoped that it would work. He badly wanted just to be around Claire. But he said, "I'm already somebody's brother. And I've never really understood the job."

"You can take the weight, Pat. You've got fabulous shoulders. Big old, strong old . . . *tank captain!*"

"Well, she's a fine lady. If she wants anything at all, she's sure welcome to come by." Patrick reflected that he had to be at the dentist by nine.

"Any horses you particularly like I could pick up for you?"

"No thanks."

"One thing I guess I better say. Big thing from my point of view, and hell, I'm a hunch player or half them wells'd still be just a star in Daddy's eye. Big thing is, I know you're cowboy enough to keep it in your pants." Tio raised his hands against any further words. "That says it all."

❖ 12 ❖

NEWS OF A FAMILY VISIT TO THE RANCH—PATRICK AND Mary's mother, her second husband and their son, Andrew—was sending Mary into one unearthly disjuncture, cycles of recollection, some assertions of a nonexistent past; and producing, for Patrick, the question, How in the world will she raise this child? He was now quite frightened; and his love for her prevented him from considering anything that would actually be a solution to her troubles. He kept on with his patchwork of concern, trying to stay available when she seemed to be slipping. His grandfather had been terrified by the barn fire, as Patrick had. And the lingering picture of the smug volunteers troubled Patrick, as though, for him, it was they who had set the fire. But then, that was a little simple, too.

When Patrick first returned to the ranch, he didn't quite know what he was doing there. Yet he couldn't look back on his years in the service as a period in which things had made much sense. His tank-driving lay somewhere between an update on a family tradition and the dark side of the moon of a highly camouflaged scholarship program. Still, he blamed himself because he had let things drift, and he now occasionally noticed that not only was he not in his teens, he was actually at an age when a certain number of people died of heart attacks. Heart attacks! He knew he was under stress but he didn't know stress of what. Maybe it was just the jaggedness-of-the-everyday. He thought of the term "stress-related" and he wondered if that was why he behaved sometimes in ways he wished he hadn't. He didn't, for example, like drinking as much as he did; yet he liked and approved of *some* drinking and the occasional comet binge with all bets off. But lately he was waking up in the dark with his heart pummeling its way through his chest and a strange coldness going through his body, waking nightmares in the dark; and he didn't know where it was coming from. He tried the trick of counting blessings like sheep, but the personal components would not cohere. He loved his sister and grandfather and horses; he loved the place. But he couldn't help thinking that it was edges and no middle. And as soon as he'd had that thought, he began to doubt it, too. He worked hard for the conclusions, then evaporated them with doubt. Worst of them all, though, was the one he called sadness-for-no-reason.

He had come home hoping to learn something from his grandfather. But the old man was still too cowboy to play to nostalgia for anyone; though as a boy he had night-hawked on the biggest of the northern ranches, had seen gunfighters in their dotage, had run this ranch like an old-time cowman's outfit, building a handsome herd of cattle, raised his own bulls and abjured farm machinery. Still, he got closer to the past in recollection: "It's not like it used to be. They've interfered with the moon and changed our weather. That's why the summer clouds sail too high to rain on our old pastures. The goddamned sonic booms have loosened all the boards in the houses, and that's why we have all those flies. Didn't used to have those. Things up there affect us. Like when you have an eclipse and the chickens fall asleep. Something happens inside and we don't know what it is. And the ground water is going in the wrong direction . . . twisting, turning sonofabitch. I had a surefire witch out here try to douse me a well for a stock tank. He said, 'I can't help you, Fitzpatrick, the inside of the world is different.' Used to be I'd have that water witch out and the bark would peel off that stick and that old willow butt would jump and buck with him and hell, we'd go fifty feet and have more gallons a minute than a guy could count." Ground water danced in his eyes.

"I thought it always changed."

"Go up on Antelope some night and look down at the yard lights. Used to be coming off any these mountains it was dark. Just throw the reins away and let the horse take you home. When that sheepherder went crazy in 1921, Albert Johanson, who was sheriff, went up to Hell Roaring and shot him between the eyes and left him. I packed in there and took the stove and tent down for Albert and then I had to put this dead Basque on a mule and pack him out. Well, it got dark. I come clean out at the west fork of Mile Creek and I could see maybe one light on the flat. But I didn't know whether I had that stiff or not till I got to Wellington's ranch and we got a lantern. I had the herder but my hitch had slipped. I had him face down on a little Spanish kind of a mule with a cross mark on his back, but the hitch slipping turned his face up, rope laid acrosst his gums like he's snarling. Old boy killed a young rancher's wife with a sickle, rancher name of Schumbert, down to Deer Creek now, older feller now. He finds this herder trying to pour cement over his wife in the cellar. Her head's set over next to the scuttle where the sickle took it off. He's so stunned the Basque taps him and he's out. He wakes up and his man is gone to the hills and his wife is waist-deep in soft concrete with her head setting on a small deal of firewood scantlings. Schumbert goes to town, notifies Albert, calls the funeral home and puts hisself into the hospital. Directly Albert goes to tracking and finds the herder's camp, just a wall-side tent and a barrel-headed horse with his front legs coming out the same hole, and old Albert, he hallos the camp. Directly here comes our Basque, packing a thirty-thirty with a peep sight, and cuts down on Albert and Albert puts him away. Then me, I'm Albert's friend. Albert has had enough for one day: He don't want to pack that camp to the valley. So I'm Albert's next victim. I hated packing that stiff because he scared the mule and all I had was a basket hitch with nothing really to lash to. When I got to Wellington's

I was surprised we still had our man, and I guarantee you this: We had that mule broke to pack *anything*. That was one mule you could call on. *God*, what a good mule." The mule had replaced the ground water and sleeping chickens in the grandfather's eyes.

Patrick saw this man, his grandfather, with no pity for himself and less for others, touching the kitchen match to a cold kerosene mantle—ignition and the wavering light on the dead man—thinking then as he would now that it was a matter of available light, a matter of seeing what one had achieved, whether one had successfully descended the mountain from Hell Roaring without losing the load, and at the same time imagining that he was illustrating a story about how there were now too many lights on the valley floor and that it was better when you had to hang the lantern in front of the spooking mule to catch the grimace of face distorted by a single lash rope crossing the mouth of a murderer and looping around the girth of a mule whose scarred flanks were decorated with stripes of blood like war paint. Had this all really disappeared?

As then, when he felt the old man's past, or when he went among the ancient cottonwoods that once held the shrouded burials of the Crow, Patrick felt that in fact there had been a past, and though he was not a man with connections or immediate family, he was part of something in the course of what was to come. None of which meant he'd failed at ambition, but only that its base was so broad he could not discover its high final curves, the ones that propelled him into the present, or glory, or death.

"How'd they get the wife's body out of the concrete?"

"Hadn't set yet."

"What'd they do with the head?"

"Propped it where it was supposed to go once they had the box. Who cares."

"What happened to the husband?"

"He wrote away for another one."

"Another what?"

"Another wife."

"What do you think happens when someone dies?"

"They can't do nothin anymore. Most religious sum-buck walkin couldn't persuade me that they can do much. Don't add up. God created an impossible situation."

Patrick thought that this was a dignified appraisal, no Ahab railing against mortality, but simply the observed, which in the end was harsh enough: that for one who could stand it, those who sought to strike the sun for an offense seemed like cheap grandstanders; and they were certainly in no shortage.

Now his grandfather took down his daily missal from above Patrick's shelf of cookbooks and pint-size bottle of sour mash, a bottle old-timers called a mickey. He sat down in the one comfortable ladder-back the kitchen had, and said, "What's for dinner?" Patrick thought, Is this our religion? He remembered a clever young tank-gunner with a year at the university who pasted the picture of a new swami above his observation port every month. He wanted war with Communism, then exciting visits to ashrams. He wanted to find himself, but first he wanted to smash Communism. He thought swamis stood for that. His name was Walt. He had records by Carlos Santana but called him by his assumed name, Devadip or something. Walt loved Santana Devadip-or-something for inventing swami rock 'n' roll. He wanted to go to Santana's hometown, but he had heard San Francisco was now commanded by fairies and therefore he thought the next thing was to smash Communism, then go on a swami tour of the Orient. Walt had luxurious sideburns that looked suspiciously as if they'd been permanented. He liked Germany but he wanted to raid the East. Sometimes when Walt's ambition had been fortified by mystery substances, especially the one he called "mother's little helper"—by all accounts something invented to keep advance-reconnaissance rangers awake for three days at a time—sometimes then Walt asked Patrick to hack a left into what he called Prime-time red, cross the border, head downtown and shell the home of the East German mayor. On such occasions Patrick referred to the gently fatal attitudes of his heroes of the Orient, urging Walt to cool his heels, at least until mother's little helper wore off. It was '76, the bicentennial. The East Germans had won forty-seven medals in the Olympics and Walt didn't like it, was real bummed out, said "Fuck it" all the time.

But that was long ago and far away, as so much eventually was. Patrick was still midway in the accumulation of his scrapbook, and paramount in that was what he thought of as a less lonely life. For now, bereft of his German girl friends and base-employed bachelorettes, the cowboy captain felt stranded on the beautiful ranch he would someday own, land, homestead, water rights, cattle and burden. He had no idea what he would do with it.

This had not entirely been necessary. There had been nice girls, beautiful girls, German dynamos with degrees who desired to be cowgirls when the captain returned, girls who could do English in the inflection of Tek-Ziz, New York or the late President Kennedy. It had been a long go on the line of the Soviet bloc and it had included paternity suits, arrangements and affection. He had tried Spain on leave, but the Spanish girls wouldn't go to the beach and the English secretaries on holiday behaved like beagles in heat at a guard-dog show in Munich. He began using an electric razor. He began not to care. He began not to brush between meals. He began to brood about the high lonesome and the girls at the gold dredge and their desire to be barrel racers and then make little babies. By now they'd had bunches of them and the babies were all in 4H. He read Thucydides and asked about soldiers' homecomings. He heard Marvin Gaye sing the national anthem at the heavyweight championship fight, and that was that. He quit the Army. He had never fired a shot, but he was going home to Montana to pick up where he left off—which was a blurred edge; blurred because of boarding school, the death of his father, the disappearance—intermittent—of his sister and the remarriage of his mother to a glowing, highly focused businessman from California who owned a lighting-design center in Santa Barbara and was a world-class racquetball player.

Now, home for a time and with no good reason to support his feeling, what had seemed the last prospect in his vague search for a reason to come home and *stay* turned out to be a subliminal inclination toward another man's wife; which was plainly unrequited if not without charm, and pointless.

Can't help that, thought Patrick. He turned his thoughts to what could be helped, most of which consisted in learning the particulars of the ranch which he had always assumed he would run but which he never had run and which, in fact, no one had ever run, except his grandfather. Patrick's father had gone off to test airplanes, and the man before his grandfather—an Englishman with the papers of a clergyman too finely scripted to be doubted by the honyockers and illiterate railroaders who settled the town—that Englishman never lifted a finger except in pursuit of Indian women and in operatic attempts at suicide in the six inches of running water from which the place was subsequently irrigated. He did leave, however, large academic oils that he had commissioned as decoration in the dining room, depicting smallpox epidemics among the Assiniboine from the point of view of a Swiss academic painter in his early twenties, eager to get home and tend to the clocks. The paintings showed all Indians in Eastern war bonnets, holding their throats in the paroxysms of dehydration, popularly assumed to be the last stage of that plague. It had never, to Patrick, seemed the right thing for the dining room. At the same time it did not deter anyone from eating. Today Patrick felt a little like the Englishman who had commissioned the paintings.

But he did have a thought. He went into the pantry, where his grandfather had hung the telephone, and being careful to stay loose, dialed and got Claire.

"Claire," he said, "this is Patrick Fitzpatrick."

"Well, hey."

"Say, I'd just remembered, I never gave Tio an answer about that colt."

"Fitzpatrick! That you?" It was Tio.

"Yes, it is."

"You callin regardin that colt?"

"Yes, I—"

"You gonna take him?"

"Yes, I'd like to."

"You should, he's a good colt. Bill us at Tulsa. Honey, you still on?"

"Sure am. Where're you?"

"I'm down to the granary with the accountants. Can you load that horse yourself?"

"Sure can."

"Carry him out to Fitzpatrick. Listen, I gotta go. Bye."
Click.

Patrick said, "Do you need directions, Claire?" He was
happy. Then Tio came back on.

"You oughta breed ole Cunt to that mare of yours, Fitzpatrick. Think on it." Click. Pause.

"Uh, yes, I will need directions."

Patrick said, "Let's just wait a second and see if Tio
comes back on."

There was a pause, and then Claire said, with a little
fear in her voice, "Why?"

"I hate repeating directions," said Patrick. His was an
odd remark. He had no such attitude. He was starting
to make things up. The last Army officer in this area he
could think of who did that was General George Arm-
strong Custer.

❖ 13 ❖

INTERMITTENTLY BEHIND THE CORRUGATED TRUNKS OF THE
cottonwoods Patrick could discern a sedan with an in-line
trailer behind it. He was replacing planks on the loading
chute, ones that had been knocked loose while he was
gone; and he could see down to the road from here, to the
sedan, the dust from the trailer and the changing green
light on the metal from the canopy of leaves overhead.
Cole Younger was the first dog to detect the car turning
in, and his bellowing bark set Alba and the hysterical Zip
T. Crow into surrounding the outfit. Patrick left the spikes
and hammer at the chute and started down the hill. Once

past the orchard he could hear the horse whinny inside the trailer and he could read the word "Oklahoma" on the plates. Was that Sooner, Hoosier or Show Me? The door of the sedan was open, but glare on the window kept him from seeing. He could make out one dangling boot and nothing else. Claire kicked Zip T. Crow very precisely and without meanness as the dog stole in for a cheap shot.

The car looked like it could pull the trailer a hundred in a head wind. Patrick had a weakness for gas gobblers; and a rather limited part of him, the part that enjoyed his seventy-mile-an-hour tank, had always wanted to rodeo out of a Cadillac like this one. He took a hard look: oil-money weird, no doubt about that. Like Australians, loud with thin lips, hideous Protestant backgrounds, unnatural drive to honky-tonk as a specific against bad early religion and an evil landscape: bracing himself against Claire.

She got out wearing knee-high boots, washed-out Wranglers, a hot-pink shirt and a good Ryon's Panama straw. Long oak-blond hair disappearing between the shoulder blades in an endless braid.

"Hello," he said. "How are you, Claire?" The dumb grin forms. No drool in the mouth corners yet.

"Just right," she said. "And you, Patrick?" There was sweetness in her inquiry. Claire just kind of stood there and let the sun hit her, only her thumbs outside her pants.

"What do we have in the back?" asked Patrick.

"Got Tio's horse."

"Aged horse?"

"Four."

"Is he broke to ride?"

"He is," she said, "but he's rank."

"What's he do good?"

"Turn around," she said. "He's real supple."

"What's he do bad?"

"Bite you. Fall on you. Pack his head in your lap. Never has bucked. But it's in him."

"How do you like him shod?"

"Just double-ought plates. Had little trailers in the back. We skipped that. He'll run and slide. He's still in a snaffle bit. You do as you like. But don't thump on him. He can get right ugly."

"Why didn't you take the horse to one of the guys around Tulsa?"

"We're gonna be here most years. We wanted to be able to see how the horse was going. Plus Tio wanted someone who was staying home with his horses." The advent of the husband into the conversation dropped like an ice cube on a sunbather's back. Could Claire have known the extent to which the horse was part of the arranging?

"How come you call him American Express?"

"Tio billed him out as ranch supplies. We named him after the card."

"Right . . . "

"Tio would give you what you wanted for your mare. You could go on and bill the accountants in Tulsa."

"She's just not for sale. But I appreciate it."

"How's she bred?" Claire asked.

"Rey Jay."

"That can't hurt."

"The only way blood like that can hurt you is if you don't have it."

You had to reach through to get the butt chain, past the dust curtain and the levered doors. Through the interstices of a green satiny blanket, the horse's color could be seen: black and a mile deep. Looked to be fifteen hands. Squeezing his butt back till the chain indented a couple

inches: a bronco. She said, "This colt can look at a cow."
She said "cow" Southwestern style: "kyao."

"I believe I'll unload him, then, and put a saddle on him
and put him before a very kyao."

She said, "If he don't lock down, give him back." Patrick thought: I won't give him back if all he can do is pull
a cart.

The stud unloaded himself very carefully, turned
slowly around on the halter rope and looked at Patrick. A
good-looking horse with his eyes in the corners of his head
where they're supposed to be; keen ears and vividly alert.

Claire looked at her watch. "Y'know what? I'm going to
just let you go on and try the horse. If I don't get back,
Tio's going to pitch a good one."

"Well, call me up and I'll tell you how we got along." A
rather testy formality had set in. The electric door at closing time.

She scribbled the accountants' address in Tulsa for
training bills and then she was gone, the clatter of the
empty trailer going downhill behind the silent anthracite
machine to the great space toward town. Patrick tried to
conclude something from the aforegoing, rather cool,
rather unencouraging conversation, then suddenly grew
irritated with himself, thinking, What business is this of
mine? I'm just riding a horse for a prosperous couple from
Oklahoma. Nobody else even knows I'm out of the Army.
I shall do as instructed and bill the accountants in Tulsa.

Patrick absentmindedly led the horse toward the barn,
trailing him at the end of the lead shank, the horse behind
and not visible to him. And in an instant the horse had
struck him and had him on the ground, trying to kill him.
Patrick cradled his head and rolled away, trying to get to
his feet, the stallion pursuing him and striking down hard

with his front feet until Patrick was upright, hitting him in the face with his hat. Patrick stood him off long enough to seize the rake leaning up against the tack shed and hold the stud at bay. The horse had his ears pinned close to his head, nostrils flared, a look of homicidal mania that will sometimes seize a stallion. It was Patrick's fault. He was in pain and he blamed himself. The horse's ears came up and he began to graze: He had no recollection of the incident. Patrick picked up the lead shank and led him correctly to the barn, the horse snorting and side-passing the new shapes in its interior, until Patrick turned him into a box stall and left him.

He hobbled toward the house, and Mary, who had heard or sensed something, came out. Patrick knew it was less than serious injury; but it hurt to breathe and he wanted to know why.

"What in the world happened?"

"New stud got me down."

"What's wrong with your voice?"

"Can't get my breath. You take me to town?"

Mary drove the Ford while Patrick scanned the road for potholes. She had some theory, some fatal Oriental notion, that this horse represented an intricate skein of influences which had already demonstrated itself to be against Patrick's best interests. Patrick couldn't help thinking that it was the horse Tio sent him.

"Mary, you haven't even seen the horse."

"That horse is employed by the forces of evil. You watch. The X-rays will show something broken."

Patrick sat on the bench outside the X-ray room, his green smock tied behind. Mary had gone on and on about the horse and its relationship to Patrick and the universe; and about how Patrick had to think about these things and not just go off and drive tanks or break any old horse or see the wrong people. Patrick sorted through his incomplete knowledge of the world's religions and, as he awaited his X-rays, tried to think just what it was she was stuck on this time. He began with the East, but by the time the nurse called him, he had it figured out: Catholicism.

The doctor, staring at the plates, said, "Four cracked ribs."

They taped Patrick and sent him home. In the car Mary said, "Now do you understand?"

"No," he said.

"There-are-none-so-blind-as-those-who-will-not-see."

"Yeah, right."

Patrick, apart from hurting considerably, disliked the monotonous pattern he had long ago got into with Mary, bluntly resisting what he saw as signs of her irrationality. He had to think of another way, though the burdens of being an older brother impeded his sense. And something about his own past, the comfort of the Army, the happy solitude of bachelorhood, the easy rules of an unextended self—some of that came back with the simple pain, the need to hole up for a bit. For instance, a friendly hug would kill him.

❖ 14 ❖

THE NORTHBRANCH SALOON IS A GRAND SPOT IN THE AFTERnoon, thought Patrick. There will be no one there, there will be the sauce in the bottles and that good jukebox. And he could start getting Claire off his mind and just sit at the bar and think about her; *then* go about his business without this distraction with her *off* his mind and his mind thereby liberated for more proper business. At this point he knew his father would have asked, "Like what?"

"Hello, Dan," he said to the bartender on duty. "George Dickel and ditch, if you would." There was a TV on top of the double-door cooler. The host was getting ready to spin the roulette wheel. A couple from Oregon stared, frozen, at his hand. Patrick gripped his drink and looked up at the "North Dakota pool cue" overhead—it had a telescopic sight; he preferred it to the "North Dakota bowling ball," which was simply a cinderblock. Claire puts her hands in her back pockets. Around the top of the bar are boards with names and brands on them. American Fork Ranch, Two Dot, Montana. There's a machine that will play draw poker against you. Hay Hook Ranch. Raw Deal Ranch. Bob Shiplet, Shields Route, Livingston, Montana. Clayton Brothers, Bozeman, Montana. I also don't think she is being accorded treatment commensurate with her quality by that Okie hubby. And what's that ailment he's supposed to have?

She could be the queen of Deadrock, like Calamity Jane, an early Deadrock great. She could be Calamity Claire. Maybe not such a good idea. Maybe bad. There were three views of the original Calamity on the north wall. In one she is dressed as an Army scout. In another she leans on a rifle and wears a fedora on the back of her head. The last is an artist's rendering on the cover of a dime novel, a Victorian heroine of the kind Patrick was crazy about.

DEADWOOD DICK ON DECK,

OR

CALAMITY JANE, THE HEROINE

OF WHOOP-UP

Oh me oh my. "Make that a double, Dan." Dan moves past the cross-buck saw, the set of Longhorns, the old-

time handcuffs, the horse hobbles, singletrees, ox yokes
and buffalo skulls; and fetches the big bourbon. I thought
whoop-up meant to get sick to your stomach. Patrick de-
clines to order a Red Baron pizza. He looks out on the
empty dance floor, the drums and amplifier, wagon wheels
overhead with little flame-shaped light bulbs. Romance.
Lost in the crowd, we dance the Cotton-Eyed Joe.
Mamas, don't let your babies grow up to be cowboys.
Hear that, Mamas? Don't let the sonofabitch happen. Lost
souls on the big sky. Hell in a hand basket.

Ease past the L. A. Huffman photos of the old chiefs
toward that jukebox, now. Get something played, vow not
to stay here too long and fall down. No sick-dog stuff.

> *Jack Daniels, if you please!*
> *Knock me to my knees!*

"Dan, triple up on that, would you?"
"Sure about that, Pat?"
"Damn sure. Got troubles."
"Well, get the lady back."
"Never had the sonofabitch. I'm just panning for gold."
"Beats wages. Beats havin' your thumb up your ass."
"You haven't dragged that triple up to me yet."
"Not going to."
"Oh dear . . . "
"Come back tonight when there's some company to
drink with."
"Oh, piss on it. Is that how it is?"
"That's how it is. You're on the allotment."
"Well, goddamn you anyway."
"See what I mean?"
"Go fuck yourself." The front of Patrick's brain was
paralyzed with anger.

"Tried all my life."

"Good-bye, Dan, you sonofabitch. I'll see you."

Patrick pulled off into the IGA parking lot, suspended in the heat against distant mountains with a special, silly desolation. He got out and walked toward the automobiles, four rows deep, clustered around the electric glass doors with labels protecting the unwary from ramming their faces.

He squeezed between a new low Buick with wire wheels and a big all-terrain expeditionary station wagon when suddenly a great malamut–German shepherd crossbred cur arose behind the glass to roar in Patrick's ear. He thought his heart had stopped. Then his head cleared. He leaned inches from the window: fangs rattled against the glass, spraying the inside with slobber. Patrick looked around and crawled up onto the hood, growling and knocking his own teeth against the windshield wipers. The monster tore around the interior in an evil frenzy, upending thermoses, a wicker picnic basket, a jerry can, clothing, backpacking gewgaws and a purse. Patrick clambered over the car until the beast's eyes were rolling; then he went inside to buy a six-pack, feeling happy among the pregrown ferns, vanilla extract and Mexican party favors. The summery youngsters seemed especially healthy as they gathered around the newest rage—alfalfa sprouts—heaped cheerfully next to the weigh-out scale, plastic bags and wire ties. As if to confirm his good fortune, he went through the six-items-or-less line with nobody in front of him but without having had any success in guessing the identity of the dog owner. So he sat on the curb and tipped back a can of Rainier while he watched the expedition vehicle. He felt a criminal tickle at the base of his neck.

In a moment an extraordinarily well groomed couple

came out with one bag and a magazine, the man in the lead, and went straight to the car. He opened it, yelled "MY GOD!" and quickly shut it. The beast arose once again in the windshield, revealing a vast expanse of whitening gum, and sized up his owners.

"Are you sure that's your car?" Patrick called out in a friendly voice.

The husband whirled. "Absolutely!" he shouted. His magazine fluttered to the pavement.

"I'd let that old boy simmer down," Patrick suggested unoffendably. The wife pertly noted that sled dogs were a little on the high-octane side.

"I can see that!" Patrick cried like a simpleton.

Something about that challenged the husband, and he pulled open the door of the car. The rabid sled dog shot between the two and landed huge and spraddled in front of Patrick, gargling vicious spit through his big, pointed white teeth.

I must be close to death, thought Patrick, feeling the Rainier run down the inside of his sleeve. I always knew death would be a slobbering animal, I knew that in Germany and I knew that upon certain unfriendly horses bucking in the rocks. It is every last thing I expected.

He did not move his eyes. The owner was coming up slowly behind the dog, murmuring the words "*Dirk, easy, Dirk*" over and over. And death passed by like a little breeze: Very slowly the lips once more encased the teeth while Dirk, double-checking his uncertain dog memory, seemed to lose his focus. The owner reached down and gently seized the collar with a cautious "Attaboy."

"Buddy," said the owner, "I feel real bad. Is there anything I can do to make it up to you?"

"I'd like some money," said Patrick.

"You what?"

"Money."

"How much money?"

"Enough for one Rainier beer in a can. And you buy it. With money."

The owner returned Dirk to the all-terrain vehicle. His wife waited, not wanting to go in there alone. The husband headed into the store, and Patrick gestured to her with the rest of his six-pack. He made her a toothy grin. "Want a beer, cutie?"

No reply.

In a few minutes, the Rainier appeared in Patrick's vision. He took it without looking up. "That fucker needs a sled."

"He's got one," the owner shot back.

"I mean your wife."

No fist swung down to replace the Rainier in his vision. All Patrick had to watch was the slow rotation of a bright pair of hiking boots; there was the sound of cleated rubber on blacktop, the door, the V-8 inhalation and departure. The high lonesome will never be the same for them, thought Patrick, however Dirk might feel. The sky will seem little.

I've been through quite an experience, perhaps the number-one Man-Versus-Animal deal for many years here in the Rockies. But I better get myself under control before it's lights out. God has made greater things to test us than ill-tempered sled dogs; God has made us each other.

WHEN PATRICK WAS FIFTEEN AND IN NEED OF REASONS TO stay in town late, he invented a girl friend, whom he named Marion Easterly. Claire reminded Patrick of Marion. Marion was beautiful in mind and in spirit. He pretended to be hopelessly in love with Marion, so that when he rolled in at two in the morning, he would claim that he and Marion had been discussing how it was to be young and had merely lost track of time. His parents, vaguely susceptible to the idea of romance in others, bought the Marion Easterly story for a year. Patrick had typically been up to no good in some roadhouse. He created a family for Marion: sturdy railroaders with three handsome daughters. Marion was the youngest, a chaste and lively brunette with a yen for tennis and old-fashioned novels about small-town boys in knickerbockers. When Patrick got locked up, Marion was never around. So gradually his parents began to view her as a good influence on their son. If he would just spend time with Marion Easterly, the disorderly-conduct business would fade, boarding school would seem less obligatory and Patrick would grow up and become . . . a professional.

In July, Patrick roped at the Wilsall rodeo, then joined the rioters in front of the bars. He'd tied his calf under eleven and was considered quite a kid, one who deserved many free drinks right out on the sidewalk. Patrick and his friends sat on the hoods of their cars until the sun collapsed in the Bridger range. By three in the morning he was back at the ranch, careening around the kitchen, trying to make a little snack. He banged into a cabinet, showering crystal onto the slate floor. A pyramid of flatware skated into fragments. He dropped the idea of the snack.

Patrick's mother and father popped into the kitchen in electric concern. Patrick reeled through the fragments in his cowboy boots, crushing glass and china noisily. He looked at them, his mind racing.

"Marion is dead," he blurted. "A diesel. She was going out for eggs." His parents were absolutely silent.

"I just don't give a shit anymore," Patrick added.

"You can't use that language in this house," his mother said; but his father intervened on the basis of the death of a boy's first love. Patrick waltzed to his room and passed out.

After ten hours of sleep ruined by guilt, booze and the presence of all his rodeo-dirtied clothes, Patrick awoke with a start and was filled by a sudden and unidentified fear. He cupped a hand over his face to test his breath, then smeared his teeth with a dab of toothpaste. He ran to the kitchen to clean up his mess; but he was too late. He really was.

His mother and father were waiting for him. The kitchen was immaculate. His father wore a suit and tie, his mother a subdued blue dress. It seemed very still.

"Pat," said his father, "we want to meet Marion's folks. We wanted to help with the preparations."

Patrick's mother had thin trickles of tears glistening on her cheeks. But they fell from eyes that were wrong.

"We can't find Easterly in the book."

"They don't have a phone."

"Could we just drive by?"

"I don't think they could handle it, Dad. I mean, this soon."

The ringing slap sharpened Patrick's sense of the moment. "*You were blotto at Wilsall,*" his mother said. "*Marion Easterly doesn't exist!*"

"Kind of embarrassing, Pat," said his father. "We went to the hospital, the morgue, the police. The police in particular had a good laugh at our expense, though the others certainly enjoyed themselves too. I'm afraid you're kind of a no-good. I'm afraid we're sending you away to school."

"It's fair," said Patrick.

"I'm afraid I don't care if it is or not," said his father. No unscheduled landings for that test pilot.

❖ **16** ❖

THIS WAS DARING BUT IT HAD REQUIRED TWO BAR STOPS: THE front door flickered open.

"Tio, where's your wife?"

"Pat, d'you just walk in?"

"I drove from my place and walked the last forty feet."

"God, what an awful joke. This your first time up here?" The effect of Patrick's joke still hung on Tio's face.

"Yes. A beautiful spot."

"It's all lost on me."

That seemed a strange piece of candor to Patrick. The ranch was beautiful, a close dirt road lying in a cottonwood creek that arose to find old stone buildings, then meadows that spread above the ranch to adjoining cirques at the edge of the wilderness. It had the quality of enamel, detailed in hard, knowledgeable strokes, a deliberate landscape by an artist no one ever met.

Somehow the handsome oilman seemed harried,

stranded on this picture-book ranch in his bush jacket and as anxious to be back among his oil-and-gas leases as Patrick had been for the loud bar.

"Claire is gypping horses in the round pen. Just go back the way you came and around the old homesteader house. You'll see it in the trees."

"I guess if I'm going to be looking after her, I'd better get the hang of it."

"That's it, good buddy. I'd fall down dead with my hand raised if I told you I couldn't get off of this vacation fast enough. You two go out and play. You can take her anywhere. She's more adaptable than a cat. All I do is dream of crude."

"You sure know your own mind," Patrick said, fishing for sense in Tio's remarks.

"Yeah, I do."

"Anything else?"

"Not really."

Claire appears to him as follows: at center in a circular wooden pen a hundred feet in diameter. Deep in river sand, it seems a soft, brown lens in the surrounding trees. Claire directs a two-year-old blood-bay filly in an extended trot around herself, the filly's head stretched high and forward, the flared and precise nostrils drinking wind on this delightful, balsamic and breezy flat.

It was on enough of an elevation that you could see the valley road mirroring the river bottom, the switchbacks to the wilderness, the flatiron clouds, the forest service corrals and the glittering infusion of sun-born seeds moving with the brilliant wind. But you couldn't see the house, and from the glade of young aspen, you couldn't see anything.

"Hello, Patrick."

"Hi, Claire."

"How are you?"

"I'm fine. Drank a bit too much, I'm afraid."

"You like this filly?"

"Sure. Isn't she deep through the heart?"

"I think she's great."

"Go for a walk with me."

"You rather ride?"

"I'm too dumb today to get a foot in the stirrup."

Claire left the longeing whip in the sand, and the filly swung gracefully forward, ears set, watching Claire leave the pen.

"Where are we going?"

"Where does this path go?"

"An old springhouse at the top of these aspens."

"I'd like to see it."

"Why?"

"I want to talk," said Patrick, "and it's easier if you keep moving, and to keep moving you need to be going somewhere."

The smallest aspens jumped up along the path with their flat leaves moving in a plane to each touch of breeze. When Claire went ahead, Patrick stared at the small of her back, where the tied-up cotton shirt left a band of brown skin.

The springhouse, now in complete disrepair, had been used to cool milk. A jet of water appeared from the ground and flowed into the dark interior of the house, gliding disparate over cold stones and out of the house again. Inside, the cold stones chilled the air and seemed to cast a dark glaze on the wood floor and sides. There was one old tree shading the house and minute canyon wrens crawled in its branches. But the wet stones were what you sensed even looking outside.

When they went inside, Patrick tried to seize Claire. Then he sat down on the plank bench, and over the water and the round river rocks their breathing was heard, as well as the catches in their breath. Patrick stared at his open hands. Claire gazed at him, not in offense or terror but in some absolute revelation. She now wore nothing but her denim pants; the shirt was in the dark stream that brightened the stones. And Patrick's face was clawed in five bright stripes. She finished undressing and made love to Patrick while his attempts to remember what it was he was doing, to determine what this meant, seemed to knock like pebbles dropped down a well, long lost from sight. He was gone into something blinding and it wasn't exactly love. Patrick supported himself on his arms, and splinters of the old floor ran into the tension of his hands. In a moment they were both shuddering and it was as if the four old windows above had lost the transparency, then regained it. And details returned: the mountain range of river stones against the wall, the electrical cord approaching from the ceiling, old saw marks and hammer indentations around the nail heads and, finally, the beautiful woman's tears running onto the coarse planks.

"You ought to get out," she said.

"What's the matter?"

"I don't do that kind of thing."

"You just did."

"I know. I bet when we're old it makes us feel lonely and empty." This could be a long, slow wreck.

They heard Tio call: "Anybody around?"

From the southwest window his distant figure could be seen trudging to the sand pen. Claire said, "I'm going straight down to the house around behind him and get a shirt. If you can think of a good cause for those scratches, you're welcome to join us."

"I wish I hadn't done that," came Patrick's contrition.

"It'll pass. It better. I'm just sick."

"Where is everybody?" came Tio's voice. Claire disappeared and Patrick followed her. About halfway down the hill, they heard him call out, "Come on, you guys! I'm getting insecure!" They rushed along in the trees. Claire was giggling.

"This makes me nervous," said Patrick as he went, realizing how preposterous the situation was.

"You shouldn't do this to me!" Tio called from afar as Patrick started his truck. Claire looked up toward the springhouse.

"He's such a little boy," she said with affection. "Listen," she added quite suddenly, "won't you have dinner with us tonight? I insist, and it's the least you could do."

Patrick drove off, thinking once again of the little walk-up in Castile, the stone counters scrubbed concave. He wondered why that came to him at these times or during summer war games at seventy miles an hour with the self-leveling cannon, the hurtling countryside on a television monitor. In the Castilian walk-up an unfuckable crone has the say of things and brings vegetables.

He cut down Divide Creek and went the back way around Deadrock. No supplies needed. Coming from this direction, you could see the ranch's high meadows cross the river bottom. You could see the old schoolhouse road and used-up thrashers and combines, drawn like extinct creatures against the gravel bank. Then this way you could run along the curving rim to the ranch itself, seeing now from above the original plan, a little bit like a fort and old-looking. Though around here nothing was really old. A woman in town was writing a book called *From Deer*

Meat to Double Wides to chronicle the area and show it was old. There was a chapter on Patrick's ranch as well as one on high-button shoes, plus prominent Deadrock families, all written at very high pitch. The ranch chapter had a romantic version of the foray against Aguinaldo's insurrection, as well as of Fourths of July celebrated with dynamite. When Patrick grew older, the ranch meant less. The trouble was, he had charged it with meaning while he was in the Army, and left without benefits. He wanted his heart to seize the ancient hills, the old windmills and stock springs. Now all he seemed to care about were the things that lived and died on a scale of time an ordinary human being could understand. Then he wanted to know what those things were there for, taking every chance for knowledge about that. Nor was he about to press his grandfather about death's nearness. But he would watch him for accidental revelations. He had a feeling that the little churches around Deadrock, all of them so different, were trying to duck this question. He was tempted to attend every one of them in a string of Sundays to see how this fatal ducking worked.

He knew that one reason he still felt so incomplete was that his father had farmed him out, left him as crow bait to education and family history. And his grandfather hadn't given his father much. All that cowboy rigidity was just running from trouble. Patrick had wandered away and Mary had flown into the face of it, the face of it being the connection they never had, an absence that was perilously ignored. The connection had not been in the airplane on the mountain; it had not even been a sign. Mary in pursuit of the ghosts was close; Claire was nearer. But he had been indecent. Had she? He was inclined to think she'd been worse than that.

❖ **17** ❖

PATRICK AND CLAIRE SAT NEXT TO EACH OTHER IN THE DEEP old leather couch. There were chunks of Newfoundland salmon that Tio had caught, in a silver bowl, and toast points made from bread Tio had baked the previous day. Then Tio brought them a superior cold pumpkin soup and pressed upon them yet another bottle of St.-Émilion before returning to the kitchen. Instead of an apron he had a worn-out hand towel tucked into the top of his tooled belt and he moved at very high speed. He said they did not have many minutes to finish the bottle and move to the dining room. Patrick was impressed. But he felt he was in a madhouse.

"Will dinner be as good as this?" asked Patrick.

"Dinner will be great," Claire said.

"And he caught these fish?"

"Oh, Tio is a sportman. Got a bunch of records and all. He shot the ninth largest whitetail to ever come out of Texas." Patrick studied her eyes, hoping he would not find real pride in the bagging of the ninth largest whitetail. He did think he saw a little pride, though. Above all, he saw the beauty of beveled face with its gray-green eyes and ineffable down-turned Southern mouth.

"How does he ever find the time to be a fine cook and record-holding sportsman?" He sensed something aggressive in his own question.

Claire looked up at him. "What else has he got to do?" she inquired.

"He's got businesses to run and a lot of money to look after."

"Tio don't have any money. *Doesn't* have any money."

"Well." Patrick was finding some embarrassment in this. Claire's amused and corrected bad English was also a moment he'd liked to have gone back over. "It seems you live well and it seems you can do as you want."

"We do. But I support Tio."

"How?"

"Inherited Oklahoma land." Stated flat. "Including mineral rights."

Patrick looked straight at her in silence.

"Tio told me," he said deliberately, "that he had a world of leases and row crops and wells he had to get back to and he couldn't mess around up here in Montana any longer."

"Tio has this little problem, Patrick."

"Which is?"

"He thinks he has those things. It's not his fault. But he gets carried away. And in some respects Tio isn't completely healthy."

"What else does he think?"

The door flew open and Tio brought in a plate of roast lamb chunks with currant jelly. He bore the mad vanity of an Eagle Scout.

"Thinks he's got a jet plane and a jillion Mexicans."

Patrick stared at Tio in shock.

"Who's this?" Tio asked.

"Guy in Houston," said Claire. She pointed toward the gulf coast of Texas.

"Oh, yeah? Well, finish them lamb and come eat dinner. It a be on in five minute."

Tio's manners and his cooking were equally fine. Yet in the tall wavering of candlelight, the conversation—ranch history and oil—carried, against what Patrick now knew, some echo of calamity, something that lingered. "You get a deal," said Tio, "to where what you're looking for is the actual lifeblood of the machine age, and this junk pools up where it gets trapped and where nobody can see it in the middle of the earth, and all we're doing is running little needles downwards toward it. Unless of course you're some old farmer with a seep. And the last one of them I know about was mounted and hangs over the dining room table at the Petroleum Club. But a man has to suspect his traps before he runs his drill in on down to where Satan is gettin out his book matches. And you got to know your domes." Then he looked around the table with matchlessly overfocused wide eyes. "I just don't care to be around people interested in other fuels. They make me sick." His eyes compressed to refocus on a forkful of perfectly prepared lamb.

"Go on ahead and eat that," Claire said quietly.

"What happened to your face, Pat? Get scratched tryin to get you a little?"

"Had a colt run through the bridle in some brush."

"Didn't know a colt had a hand on him like that."

"It was the brush that did it."

"Boy, amo tell you what, you couldn't carve a more perfecter piece of brush for that job, now, could you?"

"Say, after all this wine, I'm finally seeing what you're getting at: I try to rape some girl and she claws me. I guess I had a better day than I thought."

"Aw, good buddy." Real disappointment, moral disappointment, floods Tio's face: A man don't talk like that in company. In the flashing silence Patrick gave himself the liberty of remembering Claire beneath him, one thin arm reaching into the cool quiet, the aerial motion and breath. They ate quietly for a long time. Then he saw Tio's studying eyes deep against his own; they were, somehow, certainly not normal.

Claire got up. "I don't like to eat when it's like that."

"Food not right?" Tio asked. "Anybody says I can't cook is dumber than Ned in the First Reader."

"I'm going to sit in the living room."

"What about you, Pat?"

"I'm going to finish this good dinner."

"I'm heading for bed. I've got some studying up to do. Then me and about five of my best old buddies around the country are going to hang all over our WATS lines and make a couple of bucks."

"Well, good night, I guess."

"Good night. Don't get scratched."

"I got my colts rode earlier. What a day."

The lamb had been defatted the way they did in France. Patrick could see Tio's shadow when he came to the top of the stairs to look down to the first floor. That kind of came in intervals while Patrick went through a lot of Bordeaux. Then the shadow of Tio stopped coming and producing its simple effect. So Patrick went to the living room, where he penetrated Claire with a peculiar vengeance, noting, only at the clutching, compressive end, the ninth largest whitetail deer ever killed in Texas.

"What'd I do with my hat?" asked Patrick. "I've got the whirlies." Claire sat up, a broad snail's track on her thigh, and in her molten eyes was something Patrick had never seen before because it had never existed before, not exactly.

Patrick managed to get dressed, walking back and forth across the front of the stairs, feeling a sick and depressed giddiness, not even rememberable from the Army years, of having threaded a miserable, shivering, narrow trail to wrath and humiliation, for which he knew hell fire in one of its uncountable manifestations would someday be handed on as silver a platter as the one that held Tio's dinner. A headache set in behind his temples and he was rather in love and in a bad mood. Claire stopped him in the yard, where he walked in his socks, carrying his tall boots, staring in a dumb, fixated way at his drunken target.

Claire's small, strong hand turned him around blank by the shirt, and he looked once more into the pained eyes, forcing his own off as one awaiting a lecture. "Cruelty is something I hadn't seen in you before."

"I saw it in you. I thought I was treating you for it. I thought I was the doctor." Patrick's anger, partial product of his damages and certainly of his drinking and his indirection, formed thickly in this inconsiderate remark.

"No, I'm the doctor," Claire said. "And Tio is the patient. And you are a cruel outsider."

She walked back inside and Patrick knew which of them had lost and what had been lost. As he drove off he saw all the upstairs lights clicking on in series and he was in genuine retreat.

❖ 18 ❖

HIS EYES WERE SWOLLEN SHUT FROM THE BUTTS OF THE CUES when the chief of police shoved him into the drunk tank. "I don't know which one of you snakes bit the other first. It's all cowboys and Indians to me. But you're in my house now. And you're for sure snake bit."

"Yeah, right," said Patrick.

" 'Yeah, right,' " laughed the policeman. "Shit, you can't even talk! Look at it this way: This is probably the only bunk in town where they won't keep beatin on you. You'll get breakfast and we'll see you on home."

"I'm sorry," said Patrick, angling for the narrow bunk catercorner to one other amorphous form, foreshadowing, Patrick thought, his future. "Nothing to read. Someday I'll be a dead bum."

"I'll tell you what: You just as well throw in with me, mean as you are."

"Am I mean?"

"You're plumb mean."

"Oh, that's terrible," Patrick said in simpleminded drunkenness. "Oh, I wish you couldn't say that about me."

"Well, I can!" said the chief of police brightly.

And the lights dropped to minimum observation, just enough to get a vomiter's tongue cleared or keep some whitecross detox bozo from beating his head on the fixed steel table where, it was intended, one would eat, play cards and be polite about the finger paints. As Patrick fell off to sleep, he felt that it was a good jail, one where they preferred your being a civilian to your being a jailbird, suicide or rising crime star.

Patrick didn't know whether he was dreaming—he didn't think he was—when he heard the chief's voice, coming in through the alpha waves and alcohol, say, "The lady left your bail."

As for now, his belongings, his keys and directions to his truck were what he most required.

The note from Claire read:

> Patrick,
> Tio flew to Tulsa early this A.M.
> Stop/call for details as needed.
> Claire.

Oh shit oh god oh now what. Can this be more sadness-for-no-reason? Pig's conduct is what I'll stand accused of, you can bet your hat on that. And my feeling is that the chaps who have made such a stretch of bad road out of my body with their cues are, at any other time or place, universally considered good fellows who never reverse their cues to beat on a human and who, all agreed, had been driven to the limits of their patience and who, moreover, when the jury returned, were universally acquitted and not a little applauded by all familiar with the particulars of the case. Except that Patrick couldn't remember anything about it. Therefore he would join the cheering throng in its endorsement of each lump's administering; for though he was the recipient, democracy did call for backing one's fellows, even on limited information.

❖ 19 ❖

GRANDPA WAS DISCOVERED KNEELING ABOVE THE KITCHEN sink, killing yellow wasps against the window with the rolled Sunday Deadrock *News*. This seemed a little tough in one of our older cowboys, thought Patrick; this could be sadness-for-no-reason, although well short of harbinger-of-doom. There were dirty dishes containing glazed remains. Patrick's thought—that he'd only been gone a day —had a minute hysterical edge. What would he find with a week's absence? It seemed his grandfather had become unnaturally dependent upon him since his return. Before that, he could help, hire help, ask for help or do without. But now, silhouetted behind stacks of dirty dishes, he crawled after wasps, backlit brilliant yellow on the glass, and swung at them so hard he was in danger of losing balance and rolling to the floor.

"Did you get that editor?"

"No."

"Over to some woman's."

"Exactly."

"See you had a night in the hoosegow."

Patrick stopped. "Where are you getting this?"

Grandpa slung his legs down and unrolled the wasps'-guts-encrusted *News*. There Patrick reviewed a photograph of himself being removed from the Northbranch Saloon by the police. A lucky motorist from Ohio got the photo credit. The small crowd did not look friendly and the police looked like heroes. There was only a caption, no text; it read:

WAITING FOR RAIN

It's fair, thought Patrick.

"Well," he said to his grandfather. "Let's tidy this joint up." His heart soared with the thought of stupid little projects.

Deep in the grain bin the mice swam fat and single-minded while Patrick's coffee can sliced around them to fill the black rubber buckets. The young horses turned at the pitch of tin against oats and moved to the feed bunk, first in disarray and then in single file; and then snaking out at each other, rearranging the lineup as the yellow granules poured from the bucket.

The laminations of heat-and-serve yielded to the hot suds rising about Patrick's reddening forearms. He looked at the pleasant inflammation and thought: It proves I'm Irish. Then, with the bucket and brush, he could better see the undersides of the table as well as scrub the floor.

Here's something new: He's wetting the bed. And where does that lead? Is it a little thing, as incontinence? Or is it a nightmare with the impact of a cannon, rending and overwhelming, that would soak the tunic of the bravest grenadier? We will not soon have the answer to this. As of the here and now, we have a bed that needs changing.

At the very moment the Whirlpool goes from rinse to spin, it bucks like a Red Desert Mustang and would continue to do so if Patrick didn't heave a great rock on top of its lid, a rock that, as an interjection to its cycling chaos, restores order to as well as performs the last cleansing extraction of Grandpa's socks, underdrawers, shirts and jeans. This recalcitrant jiggling is, Patrick's old enough now to know, the deterioration of bearings and the prelude to a complete collapse—not necessarily an explosion of Grandpa's soiled linens around the laundry room, but certainly, in a year of poor cattle prices, a duskier and less fragrant general patina to this two-man operation. So Patrick views the rock as a good rock, keen stripes of marble and gneiss, a rock for all seasons.

"I have no idea what he saw. But it's sure enough undignified."

"Let me put it another way: Why did he go to Tulsa?"

"What he said was, his quail lease had come up for renewal and his father is sick, which I know is true."

"Your note said to stop by for the details."

"I guess I just wanted you to stop by!"

"Of course I *would*. And I owe you for bail."

"Anyway, what is this?"

"Damned if I know."

"It's sort of got this painful side to it."

"I know."

"Maybe nothin but ole remorse."

"Yeah, ole *remorse*."

"At least you're—whatchasay?—'unencumbered.' "

"I decided to marry my grandfather yesterday morning. As I am doing all that a wife could do for him, there's but little sense in our not making it legal. So don't go calling me unencumbered."

All of this was said, and nothing more, through the screen door of a porch, silhouettes freckled by afternoon light; they barely moved.

❖ **20** ❖

HEADING HOME, PATRICK NEARLY HAD TO GO THROUGH DEAD-rock or around it; and despite that he wanted to avoid stopping in a place renowned for its money-grubbing, bad-tempered inhabitants, a place whose principal virtue was its declining population, he needed an economy-size box of soap powder for the floors. So he went through Dead-rock. He pulled off into a grocery store where he and its only other customer, Deke Patwell, ran into each other in aisle three.

"I see I'm in the papers."

"Yup. Real nice type of fellow heading for Yellowstone. Little Kodak is all it took."

"You write the caption?"

"Sure did."

"Very imaginative."

"Thank you. How's the head?"

"Not at all good, Deke. You know those pool cues."

"Only by reputation. They say one end is much worse than the other."

"Thicker."

"That's it, thicker."

Patrick pulled down a large box of soap.

"Floors?" asked Patwell. Patrick studied the contents.

"Exactly."

"Comet's a mile better."

Patrick got a can of Comet.

"And you'll want a little protection for the knees," Patwell said, and went to the cash register with his impregnated dish pads.

Patrick followed him. "I'd use rubber gloves with those hands of yours, Deke. Dish pads are full of irritating metal stuff."

"God, I wouldn't think of forgetting the gloves. My hands just aren't tough enough with the job I've got."

Outside:

"That been a good truck, Patrick?"

"Fair. Had the heads off first ten thousand miles."

"Tell me about it. This thing's been a vale of tears. I'm going Jap."

Waves. Bye-byes. Patrick noticed, though, from two blocks away, Patwell giving him the finger. He considered it extremely childish.

❖ 21 ❖

BY FRIDAY, PATRICK THOUGHT HE'D MENDED ENOUGH TO RIDE Tio and Claire's stud. He had him in an open box stall with an automatic waterer and a runway. The horse had been on a full ration of grain all week with very little exercise. Patrick expected him to be hot. This young stallion spent most of his day looking out on the pasture in hopes of finding something to fight. When any other horse came into view, he'd swing his butt around against the planks and let out a blood-curdling, warlike squeal. So Patrick went into his stall cautiously. The stud pinned his ears at Patrick, bowed his neck and got ready for trouble. Patrick made a low, angry sound in his throat and the horse's ears went up. Patrick haltered him, took him out to the hitching rack and saddled him. He was a well-put-up horse but he looked even better under saddle. His neck came out at a good angle; he was deep in the heart girth and in the hip. Patrick bridled him with a Sweetwater bit, put on his spurs and led the horse away from the rack, got on and took a deep seat.

He rode up to a round wooden pen sixty feet across. Inside it, a dozen yearling cattle dozed in a little cluster. When Patrick rode in and closed the gate, the yearlings stood up, all Herefords, about five hundred pounds each. The stud was kind of coarse-handling, no better than cowboy broke. He smiled to think it was Claire who put this using-horse handle on him. But Patrick cut himself a cow and drove it out around the herd. The yearling feinted once and ran across the pen. The stud tried to run around his corner instead of setting down on his hocks and turning through himself. So Patrick just stopped, turned him correctly and still had time to send him off inside the cow. He set him down again in correct position. The stud reached around, tried to bite Patrick's foot and lost the cow he was supposed to be watching. Patrick didn't think he liked this horse. Nevertheless, he galloped him hard to get the nonsense out of his mind. That took two hours. This time the stud, having soaked through two saddle blankets, paid attention to his job. Patrick worked him very quietly, never got him out of a trot, but did things slow and correct.

In a sidehill above the house was a root cellar made of stone and with a log-and-sod roof. A horse fell through into the cellar one winter and Patrick built another roof, dragging cottonwood logs into place with the Ford gas tractor. He used it as a wine cellar and sometimes as a place to put vegetables if someone maintained the garden that year. In Germany he had raised tomatoes in nail kegs, and the big, powerful red tomatoes sunning on his balcony often touched his lady friends, who found the plants too piquant for words in a NATO tank captain. "You grew these?" "Yes, I did." "How *sweet*. You *are* sweet." At that point Patrick would know this was no dry run; post-coital depression was already in sight, no bigger than a man's hand on the horizon. Once Patrick picked up the nail kegs to make room for the lady, now keen to sunbathe, and midway through the effort, his face in tomatoes and vines, he said, "I'm homesick, homesick, homesick. I'm just homesick. Montana has a short growing season, but I'm homesick, just homesick . . ." After he'd done this for a while, the lady sought her dress and departed. "I don't want to see you again," she said. "Ever."

"It's fair."

Anyway, Mary headed for the root cellar to avoid a conversation, just at the moment, with the grandfather. When Patrick found her, she was moving down the rack, giving each bottle a half-turn to distribute the sediment, an almost aqueous shadow play on the ceiling, the sun reflecting on the orchard grass that grew to the cellar door. A narrow foot trail wound down the hill to the house.

"Grandpa isn't drinking that stuff, is he?"

"Once in a while. I've been cooking for him. He'll drink a little then. He seems to be taking the cure."

"Let's have a bottle of champagne."

"Very well."

Patrick found a bottle of Piper Heidsieck and uncorked it. They sat on crates in the half-light and passed it back and forth. It was nearly empty before either spoke. Mary sighed continually. Patrick felt that junkie light go up his insides.

"I'm sick of going around with my nerves shot."

"I get mad."

"Well, I get the creeps. I get bats in the belfry."

More silence. Patrick examined the sod and rafters. He decided he'd done a good job.

"Why did Grandpa try out for a movie?" Mary asked.

"He wants to be better known, I guess."

Mary said, "That's more nails on the blackboard."

"I myself would like to be extremely famous, larger than life, with souvenir plaster busts of me available at checkout counters."

"I'd like to be ravishing. I'd like to put on the dog." Her hands were shaking.

"What's the matter with you?"

"Whew . . . uhm . . . whew."

"What?"

" . . . speechless . . . "

"Here. Don't try. Have some more of this." She took the champagne. "Horse fell through. Up there. Didn't find him for two days. He ate a hundred pounds of potatoes." Mary's breathing was short and irregular. "He didn't want to leave. Then he heard the irrigating water and gave in. Didn't I build a good roof?" Mary nodded rapidly. "Anything I can do?" She shook her head. "Be better if

I leave you alone?" She nodded her head, tried to smile. Patrick left. He wanted to be quiet going down the hill. God Almighty, he thought, she is a sick dog.

❖ 22 ❖

PATRICK'S GRANDFATHER SEEMED TO BE RETURNING FROM A long trip. One imagined his hands filled with canceled tickets. It had rained a week and now the sun was out.

"Just take and put the mares with colts on the south side. Everybody else above the barn. The open mares will fight across the wire."

"I did that," said Patrick to his grandfather.

"That's the boy," said the old man, and closed the door; then, through the door: "You better look for your sister." Patrick was tall and the old man was short and looked a bit like a stage paddy, an impression quickly dispelled by his largely humorless nature.

Through the kitchen window Patrick could see his mare sidestep into the shade. The old Connolly saddle looked erect and burnished on her chestnut back. She tipped one foot and started to sleep.

"Mary's all right," he said, and went outside and mounted the horse with an air of purpose that was at odds with his complete lack of intentions. The mare, Leafy, was chestnut with the delicate subcoloring that is like watermarks. She had an intelligent narrow face and the lightest rein imaginable. Patrick thought a great deal of her. So she had not been ridden while he was away in the Army. A captain of tanks on the East German line in 1977 who comes from Montana has unusual opportunities to remember his home, and apart from the buffalo jump, where ravens still hung as though in memory, Leafy was the finest thing on the place. Downhill on a cold morning, she would buck. Like most good horses, Leafy kept her distance.

When Patrick got to the spring, its headgate deploying cold water on the lower pastures, he found Mary reading in the sun. The glare of light from the surface of the pool shimmered on the page of her book, and she chose not to look as Patrick rode up behind, leaned over and guessed she was reading one of the poet-morbids of France again, enhancing her despair like a sore tooth. Over her shoulder, on the surface of the pool, he could see Leafy's reflection and his own shimmer against the clouds.

Mary said, "Patrick, when Grandpa slapped the senator, was it something he said to Mother?"

Patrick said, "What brought this up?"

"I've been reading about mortal offenses."

"Grandpa slapped the senator for saying something about the Army, and the senator put Grandpa out of the cattle business."

"That hardly seems like a mortal offense."

"It does to an Army man."

"How do you feel?"

"Better by the minute."

"Do you miss your tank?"

"I miss loose German women."

Patrick got down and sat by the spring, holding Leafy's reins. He glanced at the book—De Laclos, *Liaisons Dangereuses*. I could very well figure out who these corrupt French bastards are, he thought, but it plays into the hands of trouble.

Patrick pulled some wild watercress and ate the peppery wet leaves, covertly looking up at Mary with her pretty, shadowed forehead. Cold water ran on his wrists.

"What are we to do, what are we to do?" He smiled.

"I don't know, I don't," she said. "We get the family this month. That will be a trial by fire, me with child and you without tank."

"I shall fortify myself with whiskey."

"The last time you did that, you went to jail. Furthermore, I don't believe your version of Grandpa slapping the senator. The Army never meant anything to him."

"Actually, I don't know why he slapped the senator."

"He slapped the senator," said Mary, "because the senator disparaged the Army. You just said so."

"And you said the Army never meant anything to him."

"That's right, I did." She looked off.

Perhaps, thought Patrick, being a captain of tanks for the Americans facing, across the wire, the captains of tanks of the Soviets has not entirely eradicated my own touchiness as to such disparagements. Although now I'm in a tougher world.

Patrick rode away. Mary turned anew to the French, and the trees at the spring made one image on the water and a shadow on the bottom. It was a beautiful place, where the Crow had buried their dead in the trees, a spring that had mirrored carrion birds, northern lights and the rotation of the solar system. It was an excellent cold spring and Patrick liked everything about it. Ophelia would have sunk in it like a stone.

When he was young, and one of the things he was managing now was the idea that he was not young, but when he was very young, a child, he and Mary picked through the new grass in the spring of the year, when you could see straight to the ground, for the beads that remained from the tree burials. Their grandmother, who was still alive then and who remembered that the "old ones," as she also called the Indians, had at the end died largely of smallpox, made the children throw the beads away because she was superstitious, superstitious enough to throw her uncle's buffalo rifle into the river on the occasion of the United States' entry into World War Two. The family had had this absurd relationship to America's affairs of war, and the Army had been a handy place of education since the Civil War. The great-grandfather went there from Ohio, and from a gaited-horse farm now owned by a brewery, only to die driving mules that pulled a Parrott gun into position during the bombardment of Little Round Top. It is said that the mules were the part he resented. Later, with the 1st Montana Volunteers, he helped suppress Aguinaldo's native insurrection.

Apart from his death, there was the tradition of rather perfunctory military service, then, starting at Miles City in 1884, cattle ranching, horse ranching and a reputation of recurring mental illness, persistent enough that it tended to be assigned from one generation to the next. Mary seemed to have been assigned this time. The luckier ones got off with backaches, facial tics and alcoholism.

The family had now lived in this part of Montana for a very long time, and they still did not fit or even want to fit or, in the words of Patrick's grandfather, "talk to just anybody." They would bear forever the air of being able to pick up and go, of having no roots other than the entanglement between themselves; and it is fair to say that they were very thorough snobs with no hope of reform. They had no one to turn to besides themselves, despite that they didn't get along very well with one another and had scattered all over the country where they meant nothing to their neighbors in the cities and suburbs. Only Patrick and Mary with her hoarding mind and their insufferable grandfather were left to show what there had been; and when they were gone, everyone would say in some fashion or another that they had never been there anyway, that they didn't fit. As for Patrick, numerous things were said about him but almost nothing to his face, and that was the only deal he cared to make.

Patrick spent the remainder of the day fixing fences at the head of the big coulee, where the ranch adjoined the forest service. In the deep shadows under the trees, small arcs of snow had persisted into the early summer. The mountains, explained his grandfather, were U.S. territory, and below them were all the people he would see in hell. There was some theater in this remark. But the old man loved his coulee. In years past they had dragged big kettles behind draft horses to make a course for match racing on Sundays, when the dirt savages were at church. You couldn't see the race, which was illegal, until you got to the rim of the coulee.

Patrick and Mary's mother, Anita, married Dale in Long Beach and had a son, now eleven, named Andrew. Anita had been in Long Beach to comfort the wife of the co-pilot, Del Andrews, after the crash. The two widows met Dale in a Polynesian after-hours club and did not speak to each other again after the engagement. Anita, Dale and Andrew were coming on the weekend. It was Friday and Mary had not emerged from her room in days. Dale had connections in Hawaii for winter vacations; but now it was summer, and once Anita got over the matter of Mary's pregnancy, they could have a super holiday in the mountains.

"If you quit carrying her food to her," said Patrick's grandfather from the stove, "she's gonna have to come out." The grandfather still made coffee like a camp cook—

with eggshells in the grounds and cold water dripping from his fingertips to make it precipitate.

"I don't believe she will," said Patrick. He had made a tray for Mary, very domestically, with French toast and orange juice. He really didn't think she would come out.

Today Mary had armed herself with the New York *Times*, illuminated from the window facing the juniper-covered slope. The light fell equally upon the nail-head bedspread and the vase of broad orange poppies from around the well pit. The room was carefully and comfortably arranged, a case of battening down the hatches. The family was coming.

Mary stopped the coffee cup at her lips, angled slightly, and said, "I don't want to deal with them, Patrick."

"It's not a matter of dealing. Don't think like that." He watched her twist up the corner of the bedspread and watched her eyes. Then the light in the room moved.

On the wall was a painting by Kevin Red Star which except for its hallucinatory colors Patrick would have liked, but which seemed, as furnishing for a troubled girl's room, to be throwing fat on the fire. More to his liking was the perfect Chatham oil, five inches across, a juniper of shadow on snow and bare ground. The blue paint from the day of the fire was cleaned up and gone.

The truth was that Mary and Patrick thought a lot of themselves at the worst of times, and of each other. This air, despite breakdowns or shooting, earned them the sarcasm of the townies. They each loved the open country where they lived, and big, fast cities. Booster hamlets failed to hold their interest. Town was for supplies.

"I didn't sleep much," said Mary. "Perhaps I should avoid the coffee so I can sleep this afternoon. What's Grandpa up to?"

"He's writing a letter of complaint to an importer of Japanese horseshoes which includes veiled references to the sneak attack on Pearl Harbor. Yesterday he was bitching about me not making my Easter duty."

"Oh, yeah? What'd you tell him?"

Mary pressed the tines of her fork into the French toast experimentally. "I said I could buy everything but the Holy Ghost."

"I'd have guessed the Holy Ghost was the only one of the three you *would* buy."

Patrick peered at her, then went down the hall and got an old Bud Powell ten-inch from his endless bebop collection. He came back, played "Someone to Watch over Me," and the two drifted off for a moment. How could a sick man like Powell bring you such peace, he wondered.

Patrick said, "I wish I could do something that good just once." Indicating Bud Powell.

"You will, now that you've picked another way of expressing yourself than tank driving."

"I sought to destroy communism."

"While despos took over America."

"Despo" was a word Patrick and Mary had—from the song "Desperado"—to describe the hip and washed-up effluvia of the last twenty years. The song itself, which now seemed to belong to the distant past, was the best anthem for a world of people unable to get off various freeways. Mary had invented the subcases: *despo-riche* and *despo-chic*.

Mary was getting jittery. Now she would ice the cake. "In bathing suits," she said, "I prefer D cups, split sizes and matching cover-ups. I love warm-up suits in luscious colors. Even though I'm expecting out of wedlock, I'm heavy into my own brand of glamour. Few days see me without intensive conditioning treatments, Egyptian non-pareil henna, manicures, pedicures and top skin-care products."

"Are you all right?" asked Patrick.

"I'm in stitches," said Mary. She began to cry but checked herself and grinned bravely.

When the record finished, Patrick asked if he should turn it over. But she gazed toward him in the concentration of someone trying to overcome stuttering, concentration or paralysis, it was hard to say.

"Try to sleep," he said. "Please try."

❖ 23 ❖

"ALL I WANT TO KNOW," SAID HIS MOTHER, "IS WHAT TRIBE?" Her eyes lifted to cut across the original buffalo grounds.

Dale, her husband, took the Igloo cooler out of the back of the station wagon, desperately surveyed the ranchstead with the rectangles of snow-line meadow between the buildings and said:

"High, wide and handsome!" His smile revealed that if no one was buying this, he wasn't selling it.

But Patrick's mother in her hearty kilt was steadfast. She locked down on tan, angular calves.

"What tribe?"

"I don't know. We will have to wait and see."

Dale said, "Anita, I thought we had an agreement about this."

And Anita said, "You're right, of course." She was still establishing Dale. Dale didn't care. His original enthusiasm had flown the coop. Now he was with his screwy fucking in-laws.

If it wasn't my mother, thought Patrick, I'd swear it was Shrew City Sue. It goes without saying that Andrew had a cap gun and that he fired away with it like a rat terrier yapping around the feet of an arguing couple. Patrick thought his mother would club Andrew, but she had turned her attention to unloading the wagon onto the lawn. Dale accompanied everything with a stream of chatter. He sensed his wife's short fuse. Dale, Patrick thought, was giving it his best. It was kind of not much.

Patrick's mother and her husband had matching snake boots. Of all the people on the ranch, it never occurred to Patrick that he in his knee-high M. L. Leddy cowboy boots and tank captain's shirt was the most anomalous. Besides that, he was now sick of America.

"Lordy, lordy," said his mother, stooping for her camera bag. "I'm going to have to control myself, if only with respect to promises I made to Dale." She'd build up Dale if it killed her.

"I think you are, Mother. Mary is a little shaky."

Dale said, "The old days seem never to have died." He wore a fixed expression memorized from a hairstyle illustration in a barbershop.

Mary's disease, if that could be said, was, Patrick thought, an insufficient resistance to pain of every kind. When she was a child, the flyswatter could not be used in her presence. Patrick watched tears stream down her face in the supermarket as an elderly couple selected arthritis-strength aspirin with crooked hands. Some of this ought to have been noticed and remembered by his mother.

The grandfather made his greetings somewhat perfunctory. After all, this was only his former daughter-in-law. His son was dead. He didn't ever pay attention to Dale and he detested little Andrew. He couldn't really understand what they were doing here. He smiled and said, "It's a big ranch. We can all damn sure keep out from underfoot if we half try."

"What's *that* mean?" asked Andrew.

"Why don't you stay out in the bunkhouse?" roared the grandfather, senility kicking in like rocket fuel.

"I think it would be nicer being near the kitchen etcetera," said Patrick's mother with a taut smile. It was clear she saw her former father-in-law as someone to be humored.

"Not a damn thing wrong with the bunkhouse," his grandfather barked. Dale started off with the bags straight for the main house, right in the middle of the conversation. Andrew was galloping, and Patrick helped with a great sagging valise that felt like it had a thick dead midget inside. They fanned out toward the house, resisting a very insistent silence. Patrick walked behind his grandfather and watched his rolling gait. Dale and his mother were in his periphery. It was a movie with the sound track gone. Andrew now bore a wretched face; his fake gun dangled at his side. For him, the West stank.

They were winding down to seeing Mary. There was the luggage, the general greeting, the formal exclamations about returning to the ranch, and then it would be faced. They rushed into the kitchen. Patrick's mother tried the cupboards; Andrew asked where he could find an arrowhead fast. Down the wooden hallway, bebop poured from Mary's room.

"Make your own," said the grandfather.

"I can't make an arrowhead," wailed Andrew. "I'm no Indian!"

When Patrick said, "Let's go say hello to Mary," a kind

of familial smile not unlike saying "Cheese" befell the little group. They followed Patrick through the narrow hall toward a drum solo coming from the farthest door.

They lost the grandfather right away. Then Dale detained Andrew. Patrick and his mother arrived as the applause began at the end of the drum solo, recorded live at the Blue Note, and the room was empty. The sheet on the bed was drawn taut, and Mary had outlined herself in ink, life-size, carefully sketching even the fingers. Across the abdomen she had traced the shape of an infant; and she was gone. Patrick went to the window; he could see across the meadow to the forest. She was either in the forest or at the spring.

"Orphanages," said Patrick's mother, "were made for good and sufficient reasons." Dale ducked his head in shame.

Then Patrick had a thought that dazed him and he panicked. He ran to the corral and caught his mare, but twisted the cinch and had to start over. Leafy felt his bad nerves and kept side-passing away from Patrick until he got a foot in the stirrup and swung up on her. She started running before Patrick could touch her with his feet, carrying him into the cold wind from the trees. Thus the ground, the sky, the vaulting motion of the horse against a static earth, seemed like life itself. The ground resisted the speed that Patrick desired, like history.

❖ **24** ❖

ONCE PAST THE COAT HOOKS, THE PLAN OF THE FUNERAL home is clear. This place can handle the lapsed of all religions. There is a corridor on the left with perhaps

three rooms leading off perpendicularly. In every one of
these rooms is someone dead. Over the door of each room
is the last name of the goner: Symanski, Westcroft, Fitzpatrick. Just at the point of division between this set of
rooms and the large room to the right, where services are
held, is a small stand holding a kind of guest register; it
has an attached light. A discreet brown cord trickles over
to the wall outlet. The owner stands behind the guest
book and flags the dalliers by the coatrack; he is dressed
somberly, but not grimly. His is the air of riding out a
good franchise. Here and there are his assistants, that odd
breed of Recent Graduates in smart suits and razor-cut
hair who have decided to spend the rest of their working
lives driving hearses and standing in attendance at funerals
with their hands just so.

Patrick, the blood rising in his head, circled past the
casket with the other mourners; he took one look at the
barbaric effigy constructed from his deceased sister and
decided: I have no attitude toward this. He was still far
from knowing what had happened to him.

They sat in the front row: Patrick, his mother, Dale, his
grandfather and little Andrew. Little Andrew had wanted
to touch the body. He got a good snatching for that. The
grandfather gaped around and smiled at his contem-
poraries, all of whom, Patrick felt sure, were thinking:
Odd for a person so young to go when it's usually one of
us. Patrick wondered if these old people didn't feel a little
edge, thinking time was not so reliable a force against the
living that it could be utterly counted on. There was always mishap, the unexpected; and in this case, the perils
of one's own hand. Few had the nerve for that and, all in
all, went uncounted, as they were easily dismissed as
mental cases. The old people gazed around: this was just
social. Of course, there was death. The middle-aged

worked on the theater of doom, many of them with dramaturgical mugs that wouldn't pass muster at the local playhouse. The very young craned around like the very old; and all were surrounded by the funeral house staff, including the altogether depressing Recent Graduates. Patrick was getting angry. Mary was gone and this bit of drill seemed superfluous. Moreover, the audience included a substantial group of townies eager to see the family on its knees, which Patrick could have stood for, except that there was no family anymore. The mother was divorced and gone, Patrick was in disgrace, his father long dead, his sister was ridiculed before she died; and his grandfather despised everyone. Patrick was growing more incensed by the second.

The Ford dealer bowed his way down the aisle, holding a narrow-brimmed and piquant fedora, obsequious before a couple of hundred prospects. His wife stared into infinity, her cylindrical hat indicating a level stance in the face of mortality. A tiny wino brakeman slipped in because he'd seen the gathering. The preacher materialized in the wings, counted the house and withdrew to await the swelling crowd. Deke Patwell was on hand to report the loss. A lip reader from the stationery store sat front and center with her own missal. The song "Chapel in the Moonlight" came dimly from invisible speakers. There were five Indians with hard Cheyenne features, two of whom were young enough to be suspects as Mary's paramour. Andrew had a cast-metal articulated earthmover, which he rolled quietly back and forth between his feet. His mother moved her shoe to block its progress and Andrew looked up at her with no expression whatsoever.

Scattered around the audience were people never before seen in town, friends of Mary's from all over the

Rockies. They were uniform in age but staying well away from each other.

The minister began to move under the arcade of flowers past the casket toward the Recent Graduates pushing the lectern at him from the opposite direction. "Chapel in the Moonlight" diminished and disappeared. Patrick's mother drew back the silk string from her missal and raised the face of one who, as the mother of a suicide, had nowhere to hang her next glance. Dale seemed to be saying, This is how it is.

The minister gazed for a long time at his own little volume; and when the moment came at which its pages could best be heard, he turned it open, gazed, then abruptly closed it again: he would speak from the heart. That was a good one, and everybody looked at him, even the Recent Graduates, sharpening expressions in anticipation of something daring.

"Young Mary Fitzpatrick," he crooned, "was a free and delightful spirit . . . " He paused. Perhaps he never should have paused, or paused so long, because the fury Patrick had feared arose in him and he spoke.

"*Shut up,*" said Patrick in a clear voice. "*We knew her.*" The quiet was like undertow.

The minister's head fell with patience. Patrick arose. His mother's face turned in horror. Nearly half of the audience got up and started to the rear. The editor-in-chief gazed back at Patrick, then led the group out. Aaron Clark, the prosecutor, stayed close alongside the editor. Dale, after a moment's reflection, left with them. Patrick's grandfather pulled Andrew onto his knee. The Indians milled and went, leaving one frightened young man in a Levi jacket and carrying a broad-brimmed uncreased straw. That's our man, thought Patrick, but I won't talk to him. It's all disgrace. Patrick walked up to the minister and demanded to know where he had gotten the business about the free and delightful spirit. "You never met her. That was an unhappy girl and she isn't going anywhere. She's just dead." What remained of the audience stirred at this ghastly speech.

Patrick turned to go and spotted the Indian. He changed his mind about talking to him. They looked at each other hard and Patrick asked him to wait outside. Patrick watched him turn slowly and go into the blind light at the door, affixing the straw hat as he did so, causing a sudden deep shadow to reveal his face as he stared back in the glare, his expression very much that of something cornered and awaiting necessity, grave and shy at once.

"Have you had enough?" He saw his mother. He was blank. "Have you had enough, I said! I *said*—"

"I heard what you said." She was right into his face. He gazed off at the casket and thought about that Indian in the sidewalk glare, the angular, expressionless face lit by the dark under his straw hat. "You said nothing."

Between the pews Patrick's grandfather led Andrew to the rear. The old man looked upon Patrick with a sadness he'd never allowed to be seen before. Patrick couldn't understand the expression at all, not at this time.

"Take it easy, Pat," he said. "I'll bring little Andrew here. It's just best for you to go on out of here. Andrew wants an arrowhead. So I'll try to find him one. And then they're going to bury her, see. And what I'm saying is it's just best if you go on out of here, Pat."

"Did you happen to notice the newspaper editor?" His mother inquired. She walked off, leaving no time for a reply, though in an instant of stunned, relieving giddiness, which shot through his grief like a tiny spark, he almost told her that he read only the sports page. Then he thought of his grandfather and walked toward the light. He knew and felt the people's close watch on him. He had always understood that to observe the burying of other people's dead was one of the few things that made their lives palatable.

But best of all the agony of those who remained. Aha! There had not been a good death like this one in Patrick's family for some time. His father's death in the desert of the Great Basin had seemed remote. There had been a dry spell. But Patrick knew, too, that he had not learned; his grandfather had walked out and given them nothing. There was nothing in the old cowboy's face, his straight-backed walk toward the door, to give them anything. And Patrick had raved. He had raved for nothing. So this was a good one. This was one of the best ones they had ever seen.

❖ 25 ❖

THE INDIAN WAS ON THE SIDEWALK, CARS DISAPPEARING fast around him. He dropped his face slightly at Patrick's appearance in the door and then looked once behind him. Patrick saw something guarded and ready in his stance, the clear, round, pale brim intersecting his delicately modeled forehead.

"Do you need to see me?" Patrick asked.

"If there is something between us."

"What's that supposed to mean? Is that Indian talk?"

"I don't know."

"What's your name?"

"David Catches."

"Well, they're going to bury my sister. Will you be going?"

"You'll make another speech. I don't want to hear that kind of thing."

"Then why don't you come to the house tonight?"

David Catches followed a police cruiser with his eyes as it rounded the corner and vanished at low speed.

"What time?"

"Before the sun goes down and we lose our light. That way we won't be stuck inside. Do you know the way out there? Do you know how to get to our place?"

"Of course. I helped your grandfather."

"I guess I knew that."

"You were in the Army. At that time your grandfather didn't take care of himself. I didn't have any rattles. I had a Goldenrod fence stretcher and a slick-fork saddle. Mary brought me there to make him an Indian. I punched cows and peeled broncs for a couple of years. But I saw a way to get out one night and I was gone. I got away just before I learned to think like him."

An old man walked by, leading matched springers. He walked his dogs according to the National Bureau of Standards, so that people could set their watches by him. In Deadrock there were children who thought one told time by dogs.

"When did all this occur?"

"We went to Grassrange and I worked for an Indian who ranched on Flatwillow Creek. A guy sent me some horses to break, from over at Sumatra. Mary came with me! We had a trailer house down in the trees. We had a good dog and four good saddle horses. We were happy. Then something must have gone wrong. Anyway, Mary was gone, one day just gone."

"She turned up in Roundup."

"I don't know."

"Then on down to Warm Springs. Hey, I'm giving you the details."

"I just don't know."

A silence fell over them, an unresisted silence like a trance. Then David Catches said, "You've got to go now. I will see you tonight." To Patrick it seemed a moment later that the silence resumed. Except that this time an arrangement with straps and pulleys lowered Mary into the earth between panels of artificial turf that covered the scars that the machinery had left making the hole. Only the family was there, and since Patrick was responsible for the absence of the priest, it was felt he should say something by way of a benediction. He said, "I'll never see her again."

It required three cars to carry the family. The cars were parked down on a blacktop crescent below the mausoleum. You could see the foothills from here and a few farm buildings along the base of the escarpment, like curious physical interjections in the landscape. Patrick viewed this all helplessly as Mary's habitat, knowing that on this broad hill, picked for its view, gale-driven snow stretched immense drifts toward the west, over everything, over stones and monuments, and that there was nothing that could be done for that. On the upper end of his own ranch, a miner had, years ago, filled coffee cans with cement and pressed marbles into its surface, picking out the name of his three dead children. So anyway, except that there was nothing new in this, it was the one thing that was always new.

26

IT WAS PITCH DARK. "I AM MARION EASTERLY," SAID THE voice. "You never let me exist. I am not allowed to let you rest. But one night at the proper phase of the moon, a neither-here-nor-there phase of the famous moon, I will arise in the face of our mother and our father and I will be real and you will not have been sent away to school and the proper apologies will be made and you still will have won the roping drunk at the Wilsall rodeo; and all, all will be acceptable." Patrick turned on the bedside lamp and there was Mary, grinning and buttoned up in a navy pea-coat. "Take away the offending years," she said, "for they have ruined us with crumminess and predictability."

"Go to bed," Patrick said to Mary. "Anyone can see you've gotten yourself altered."

Dale turned around in his front seat to look straight at Patrick. The driver, never seen before, presented himself as a concerned friend of the cemetery franchise. He offered to drive and they let him. The other cars were driven by concerned friends of the cemetery as well.

Dale said, "That was quite a deal you put on, Pat."

"How long did it take you to pump yourself up to say that, Dale?"

"No time at all." By his own scale, Dale was dauntless.

"Well, if my grandfather would have the courtesy to die, it might mean something to you, even as a lease deal. Why don't we pull the other car over and find out just how long Grandpa is going to pull this business of not dying?"

"Stop this," said his mother. Patrick's batty conduct made her practical.

"Driver, detain that car."

The driver said, "This isn't a patrol car."

"I say stop that car. Remove the offending mystery."

Dale said, "This will not continue."

"My father is dead as well," said Patrick. "But he's no use that way, is he? He's no use to Boeing aircraft and he's no use to us— Driver, pull that car to the shoulder. I accuse its occupant of lingering."

Patrick could tell that he was ignored like a bad drunk. Beautiful scenery rolled past the windows and was of absolutely no use or comfort to anyone. He looked over at his mother, stranded in horror, and thought, What is the use of my going on like this? And there is no repairing what I've done, nothing to be helped by apology. No use.

But when he got to the ranch, he was quite astonished to see the broodmares pasturing the deep grass, their foals moving like shadows next to them, twisting their heads up underneath to nurse. That was one thing that seemed to go on anyway, something that helped, unlike the baleful and unforgiving mountains. He thought, I hope Andrew will find an arrowhead. And if he doesn't, that Indian will make him one, if he's any kind of an Indian.

What could I have done? I might well have canceled the reproving-older-brother performance. I might have done better than that. And was there anything to the remark heard over the years that Mary had "that look," that she was doomed? We shall quiz the Indian as to doom. We are encouraged to think they are the only ones with coherent attitudes on the subject. It's the world-wide aborigine credit bureau.

The dinner table was set and there was food. Patrick didn't know how it got there and he had no idea how the five people converged at the same time while the late-afternoon sun blazed through the windows. It was clear that no one but Andrew was going to do anything with the food. Funeral meats, thought Patrick. Where does that come from? I'm afraid of the thought.

"How do you like that dinner?" he asked Andrew.

"It's great," said Andrew. "Except for those things, those Brussels sprouts."

"Well, eat up."

"Gonna."

Then Patrick's mother began to sob. She sobbed bitterly and deeply, as though a convulsion was at hand. Dale looked across at Patrick. "Are you happy?" he asked. Patrick shook his head. He was wrong again. Dale wasn't even gloating.

"Aw, come on, Mama, please stop," Patrick heard himself say.

". . . can't . . ." In her grief she looked strangely like Mary.

"It's over. Nobody could do anything."

"It isn't true," she choked. "It's not."

Andrew looked from face to face, as if he were at a tennis match. Dale stood up. He wasn't an impressive man, but he seemed to have a right to his disgust.

"I'm going to the bunkhouse," he said. "I'll have the car ready in a bit. We're going to leave immediately." He turned to Patrick. "*What have you and your sister done?*"

"What have my sister and I done!" Patrick repeated in an astonishment that faded easily.

Dale lifted his wife to her feet. "There are things you don't do. Andrew, let's go." The pale lighting designer had gotten indignant. Patrick felt an odd strength in it.

"I'm still eating!"

"We'll stop on the way. Get up!" Andrew raised his

hands and shrugged philosophically. Then he stood. When
the three went through the dining room door, Dale had
one more thing to say: He said, "You've shed all of it
you're going to on my wife. It was an old trick of your
father's. But don't you start."

Dale left, crazily brave in his elastic-waist vacation
pants and loud shirt. Patrick did note that he stood up for
his own. And what do I stand up for? You better think of
something fast.

❖ 27 ❖

PATRICK'S GRANDFATHER, MASHING PEANUT BUTTER ONTO AN
unheated English muffin with the back of a spoon,
watched a wasp cruising the honey jar and asked Patrick
if he wanted to unload the ranch. He was sure that a
pigeon in the form of a deer hunter from Michigan would
appear.

"What else would we do?"

"I don't know. Get on out of here maybe."

"It seems like I just got back."

"We could go to the Australia."

"I don't think so."

"Country like this used to be. No sprinklers, no alfalfa,
no yard lights, no railroaders, no nothing."

"I don't know," said Patrick. "I don't want to go to
Australia." He visualized Limey prison descendants pho-
tographing koala bears in vulgar city parks.

"This country used to be just nothing and that's when it
was good. And they say the Australia is one big nothing.

I'm telling you, Patrick, I bet we'd do good out there. You can run a spread with just your saddle horses."

Then it got quiet again. There was nothing further to be said about the Australia. There was not even anything to be said about the departing station wagon, whose lights wheeled quickly against the house.

"Tell me about David Catches," said Patrick.

"Oh, yeah. Well, he was here for a while. It wasn't right, but your sister had him here and he was of some use."

"What kind of use?"

"He was good with stock. Worked a long day. But then after that was done, he'd try to tell you how it was. I think Mary made him do that. I don't think he wanted to."

"What did you do about it?"

"I told *him* how it was."

"How long did this go on?"

"Couple years."

"How come I never heard about it?"

"Like I said, I didn't feel it was right. I mean, here's this Indian. And what was Mary up to? I just didn't feel it was my job to explain it."

"Maybe it is." That's what the jailer thinks, thought Patrick: Throw in together and save the world.

"Anyway, he went to making an Indian out of me and it wasn't in the cards."

"Why did he try to do that?"

"He had Mary about halfway made over and I guess he figured to start in on me."

"Did you believe any of it?"

"Some of it."

"Like what?"

"I don't know."

"I mean just for instance."

The old man twisted about. "Well, Patrick, this guy'd give you the feeling he'd know where Mary had gone." Now there was absolute quiet. In a moment the old man spoke again: "Pat, what you said today did not absolutely one hundred percent wash with me." Here it comes.

"Well, I don't know. I don't know if I've ever done anything right anymore. I already feel a little bad about the way they left out of here. Do you feel good about anything anymore?"

"I feel good about the Australia and the movies."

"Come on."

"Well, I like what I had, the way I used to live. There's nothing to do anymore, but I'm too old to do much anyway. I can go out in the hills, but I got to take a horse I'm a hundred percent sure won't buck me down. Who wants to go in the hills on a horse like that? So I think about something I know for certain, like how it once was for me, like when I nighthawked on the Sun River. Or I think about something I don't know one thing about, like the Australia. And that works pretty good. I recommend it. I say it's good. I'm not saying it has to be the Australia. It could be just an animal you've never seen." The old man changed his gaze. Patrick turned to see David Catches in the doorway, his hat removed and held with both hands, his black straight hair swept back. Catches smiled and nodded. "You could think about that Indian," the grandfather continued. "I don't know any more about him than I do the Australia." Patrick got up from the table.

"Be back in a sec, David, I've got to get a few things." Patrick hurried off down the corridor.

"You been staying busy?" asked the grandfather.

"Pretty much."

"Doing what?"

"Punching cows."

"Where's this at?"

"Different places. Roundup, Ekalaka, Grassrange, Sumatra. Different reservations. Up on Rocky Boy."

"I'm hardly ever horseback," the grandfather said angrily. "Time was, irrigated ground was considered modern."

Patrick walked in. He was carrying a small valise. His grandfather went to the window.

"Are we ever going to eat?"

"I don't want to."

"Catches, what about you?"

"I stopped in town and got a hamburger."

"You know what I can't remember?" asked Patrick. "Whose idea was it we talk?"

"I don't know," said Catches. "Doesn't matter. What d'you got in the sack?"

"Whiskey. Number-one kind of bourbon."

"Okay," said Catches.

"That way we've got a shot at some actuality, medicine man. I mean, this isn't going to be the sweat lodge."

"You're not gonna do your well-known mean-drunk thing, are you?" asked Catches. Patrick gave him a long look.

"All it is, is for loosening tongues and to make sure we don't have any mystical ceremonies."

Catches put his hat on and walked over to the sink. He twisted the faucet, cupped his hand under the stream, drank, turned off the water and wiped his face. "No more cracks. I tried to save her too."

Patrick sat down. "Save her from what?"

"You people and her own thoughts."

"I don't want to talk about this," said the grandfather.

"Stay where you are," Patrick ordered. "Have a seat,

Catches." Catches drew a chair with the same fatal gesture he extended to the hat. Now the hat was foursquare on his head and he was looking at the whiskey Patrick unloaded on the table. The yellow electrical light contained the three of them in the dying day. Catches couldn't keep his eye off the bag. Patrick filled a jug with cold water and set three glasses on the table. He filled the glasses nearly full with whiskey. "The ditch is in the jug, boys. We're all throwed into this mess. So make yourself brave."

Catches tilted the whiskey back to his face and, pausing very momentarily, produced a wicked little knife from its leather encasement, a narrow blade with dark, oxidized steel, a maple handle with stars and silver faces. He didn't seem to mean much by the gesture.

"Is that anything special to you?" Patrick asked. His grandfather got up and walked out. "Spooked the old boy. Well, is it?" They could hear the grandfather slamming doors down the hallway.

"Just a little knife. I cut binder twine with it."

"Uh-huh."

"Do you think you helped Mary an awful lot, being an Army officer who kind of looked down on her no matter how much she thought of you?"

They drank another glass of whiskey before Patrick answered: "Is that what happened?"

"You didn't save her. I am saying that."

"Maybe *you* should have saved her," said Patrick. "And I didn't look down on her. I neglected her. It's different."

"You didn't do jack shit."

"This is a pretty state of affairs," said Patrick. "Who's to pour our whiskey?"

"I'll do it." Catches refilled the glasses.

"I have something you can take to the powwows," Patrick said. "You'll be the talk of the town." He left the room for a moment.

It was the sheet Mary had painted of herself and the baby. He draped it over the shoulders of David Catches.

"This was Mary's way of saying, '*Adiós, amigos.*' I want you to have it for whatever gala occasions you chaps have down on the reservation, social events that inevitably produce the Budweiser flu and well-known Cheyenne jalopy crashes. Having said that, we will now drink heap more deathbed whiskey. You didn't take care of her."

"What care could you take of her? She was a grown woman." Catches stopped. "Besides, we are now to the place where one of us is inclined to kill the other."

Patrick moved very slightly in his chair.

"On the basis of what?"

"On the basis of two men revenging themselves upon each other for what they haven't done themselves. Boy, I don't know what that means."

"You came close."

"I know," said Catches, "but I fell on my ass."

"More sourmash for my lieutenants," said Patrick. "Away with the offending mystery."

"As you wish."

"Catches, are you an educated man?"

"I certainly am. Let's drink at high speed."

"Okay."

"We have a shot at murder tonight. I'll wear this sheet to remind me of your insult."

"I think that would be appropriate."

"What do you have for a weapon?"

"I have my skinning knife," said Patrick.

"Get it," said Catches.

"I am in considerable pain." Patrick found his skinning knife in the hallway. It had a deeply curved blade and a worn birch handle.

"Not a bad knife," said Catches.

"It is designed," said Patrick, "for disheartening an aborigine."

"But what's at issue?"

"Oh, dear. The noble savage displays his vocabulary. At issue, let me see. At issue is whether you caused Mary despair."

"I thought it was like flu."

Patrick stared at this arrogant Indian whose infuriatingly expressive hat drew a jaunty line above his eyes.

"What do you think about us getting drunk?" Patrick asked.

Catches said, "A warning has come to me that there is no escape."

"I've had no such warnings. Everyone hears footsteps. But no sacred eagles bearing messages."

"How much of that is there left?"

"Another bottle."

"Brought out this sheet, did you?"

"How do you like the fit?"

"A little long in the back."

Patrick asked, "Do we each have a fair chance?"

"Depends," said the Indian. "But not if it's up to me."

"Last Indian I remember making the papers was a Northern Cheyenne named Paul Bad Horse who killed that supermarket clerk, cold blood, for what was in the till. Paul wasn't charging the cavalry. Paul got our clerk in the back of the head."

"Stop this small stuff." They topped off water glasses with brown whiskey. Patrick thought, This Cheyenne is going to buckle under the sourmash. He thinks he's got something for me to buckle under; but it's going to be a cold day in hell. I'm going to ice this redskin.

"See, where you're just exactly one pickle short of a full jar, Tank Captain, is that you think you're going to come to me as my equal in matters concerning Mary. Besides, you are less educated a man than me."

"She's dead and we're not."

"Neither of us is wily," said Catches. "Neither of us is getting paid to do this— Give me a refill . . . thanks. But if it went just right, one is prepared to kill the other. We should have a complete agreement about that."

"I think that's real fucking boring and obvious."

"I can't help that."

"We can't bring Mary back."

"No, we can't," Catches began, tears gleaming down his face.

Patrick's grandfather appeared in the kitchen doorway dressed in his long johns. He was in a red-faced rage.

"I'd like you two to go. All right? Go away. Go to the barn. Go anywhere. Go away. I've listened to as much of this as I will. It's terrible. *It's terrible what you both say, pouring that out.* But on this place the answer is no. Take it away, take it to such-and-such a place, but get it out of here."

The two younger men went outside. It was a cold night and the stars crowded down upon them, the buildings of the ranchstead scarcely visible in their light. Patrick was utterly lacking in anger. All he wanted to say was the right thing. "Don't know just where to go here. David, you bring the bottle?"

"I got it."

Patrick thought he could see him gesture with the whiskey. They were already drunk, and Patrick had it in his mind to get down to a thing or two if he could think just what those things might be. Then it struck him with a shock that it might have been no more than that he was still trying to get close to Mary.

"Let's get us a couple of horses," said Catches. "Ground's all beaten down around here. We'll get up in those hills. We've got one and a half bottles of whiskey to go."

"Nobody says we have to drink it all."

"Only that's what's going to happen."

They'd already diverted toward the corral, where the barely shifting shapes of horses moved at their sound. There were stars over the horses' backs and you couldn't see where their legs reached the ground. When his mare Leafy turned to him, though, he identified the space between the glints her eyes made; and the sound of her relieved exhalation at recognizing his approaching shape helped Patrick sort the horses.

"Here's my mare. Why don't you go in there and grab that claybank? I'm supposed to been riding her more." Patrick saw Catches' halter flip up around another horse, a bay.

"I got one I broke."

The two saddled up in the deeper darkness in front of the saddle shed. Patrick could hear the steady, rapid preparation of Catches, the heavy noise of the saddle slung up on the bay's withers, the slapping of billets and latigo, then the tight creak when he cinched up. They swung into their saddles and each rigged a bottle against the swells with the saddle strings. Catches still had Mary's sheet.

"North Fork suit you?"

"That'd be fine," said Catches.

"What do you carry that little knife around for?"

"You know Indians: homemade tattoos, drinking and knife fighting."

"That kid Andrew wanted an arrowhead. You might have got him a yard rock and chipped on it a little."

"I was relaxing at a dinner party," said Catches. "Life is more than just work."

Remove the offending silliness, Patrick thought. Make it all fair. But then he felt even sillier. They went through three or four gates before they hit the forest service trail, trickling up through the trees in the starlight while Patrick felt sillier and sillier, looking back every now and again to see the floating white shape of Catches' hat above the dark form of the moving horse.

"I like this whiskey, David."

"You bet."

"I like it in bars as well as out here in the widely promoted high lonesome."

"Right, Patrick."

"But in the bars—watch that deadfall—but in the bars, a fellow tends to act up because of the social pressures. After you act up once, you're expected to act up again. Grown men on crying jags, pistoleros wetting their pants—" An owl fled rapidly up the trail on beating, cushioned wings, and they watched it go. "I would like to build myself a big stroller," Patrick continued. "Like babies have, y'know, shaped like a doughnut with a sling seat in the middle. Wheels that let you go in any direction. It would have drink holders and cups for poker chips. You could just scoot around and not worry about falling."

"That's quite an idea. You ought to write that down. Yeah, I'd get that one on paper."

The air currents changed and then the smell, cool and

balsamic, came from the high draws in the darkness on either side of them. Sometimes when the trees were closed solidly overhead and they moved in absolute blackness, Patrick could tell the direction of the trail only by feeling the mare's body turning beneath him. When the trees opened once again like a skylight, Patrick stopped and offered Catches the bottle. Each of them took a deep pull, rerigged the bottle to Patrick's saddle and moved on. Patrick inhaled deeply through his open mouth, carbureting the sourmash and piny air into a powerful essence. A peculiar feeling rose through him, seemingly a glimpse of time's power: roping, soccer, Germany, the ride on I-90 with Mary, even the fine mare creaking underneath him. Then that evaporated and the Indian floated behind him on the bay.

"We could use a couple of those strollers you mentioned," said Catches. "Perfect for going down the mountain."

"One time when Mary and I were small—"

"Look back at those lights."

"I know. One time when we were small—"

"See how they drop into the groove the trail makes as we go up? There's only four left. Now three."

"Then can I tell my story?"

"Okay."

Patrick kept riding until the last ranch light dropped into the trail.

"We shared the same room, see. And my folks came back back from a party at Carlin Hot Springs. And they were having words. Well, my dad gets out his duck gun and blows away the plumbing under the kitchen sink. They used to just endlessly do stuff like that, you know, really hating each other. And we'd lie in bed thinking, Please don't get divorced, please please please. That and the atomic bomb were our big scares. So anyway, the water is running everywhere and my grandfather comes in, smacks my father in the face and disarms him. So my mother just shrieks at my grandfather, who's trying to fix the plumbing. My father keeps saying, 'Sorry, Pop, sorry.' And pretty soon my mother comes down to our room and opens the door. The water was right behind her. She turns on the light and sees we're awake. She's real drunk, but she gives us this long looking-over. Then she announces, 'Why don't you two just get out? Why don't you just get the hell out and quit causing all this trouble?'—How's that for a family tale?"

"I thought your dad was supposed to be so terrific."

"Well, we're up here on a truth mission, aren't we? He wasn't so terrific. But when your father dies he becomes terrific through the magic of death." Patrick thought, with releasing clarity, Especially when he falls out of the sky in flames. Wow and good-bye.

"Y'know," Patrick mused, "some things are like a watershed. They mark between the before and the after."

"Name one."

"Like the first time . . . the first time you put your shirttail between the toilet paper and your ass."

"Aw, for crying out loud."

Then Patrick thought what he really meant and his throat hardened and ached and it was necessary for some time to ride in silence to combat sorcery and recollection through the metronomic sound of horses.

They dropped down into a swampy spot, the horses drawing their feet heavily from the muck; and as soon as they stepped up the other side, they woke a half-dozen blue grouse, who thundered off and scared the horses into staring and motionless silhouettes. Then once again they were going.

"If it was daylight, we could've shot a couple of them to eat at our powwow."

"Do you have a gun?"

"Nope."

God Almighty, Patrick was thinking, I am indeed away from the tank and must, as I had said I would, begin anew or at the very least go on to the next thing undaunted by either failure or death, neither of which I have mastered, though I cannot be accused of facing them with fear; but what did you know about them, relieved in fear at the arrival of adrenaline, relieved in death at the arrival of the embalmed dummy, relieved in separation by the dazed and unremitting sense that there had never been connection, not with people and not with places? What had Germany been? Three or four colors, twenty vulvas and strudel? Growing up, as life blind-sided you with its irreversible change, the heart pleaded for rituals that would never come: the West, the white West, a perfectly vacant human backdrop with its celebrated vistas, its remorseless mountains-and-rivers and its mortifying attempts at town building. Patrick longed for a loud New York bar.

"When they reached the slope where the ranges divided, it looked like an enormous open lawn in the dark. There were the shapes of animals out on this expanse, deer or elk, and those shapes drifted away as Patrick and David picketed their horses, then sat facing the slope that elevated darkly to sky. Stars disappeared as the black shapes of clouds cruised the bright space. And for a while, all you could hear was the drinking.

"Had this cat living in the trailer at Grassrange," said David. "Could walk upside down on the acoustic tile all the way to the overhead light and kill moths and eat them and, y'know, like let the wings stick out of the corners of his mouth up there next to the light."

"Think the glare would get to him."

"He wouldn't even take his shot. Just hang there alongside the bulb and prettyquick a moth would fly into his mouth. Fat sonofabitch and I never seen him mousing during moth season. Then in the winter he'd move out of the trailer into this Amoco barrel used to be a dog's house there at Grassrange and hunt mice. He snagged one bat at the light in two summers; otherwise, it was all moths. He had to get down on the floor and fight that bat, though."

"What did Mary do while you were there?"

"She'd just be reading, mostly; cooking. Then people'd bring her young colts to halter-break and gentle. She had chickens. She took a lot of pictures of that cat on the ceiling, but we never had the money to get them developed. I could drop the film by, if you're interested. I mean, if you felt like getting them developed. Mary was afraid the light bulb would overexpose the film and we'd've spent our money on nothing at all. Really, we didn't have no money." Catches started crying.

"Jesus Christ, David."

"I don't know."

"Come on now."

"I just don't know."

"Sit up there, old buddy. I can't stand it. Come on, now, you're gonna get me going."

"Well, what's the fucking use?"

"I don't know."

"What's the use?"

"There isn't any use. I thought Indians knew that."

"Somebody steered you wrong, Fitzpatrick."

"Well, you better figure it out. There seems to be signs everywhere that there's no use."

"Spoiled my fucking hat tipping over on it."

"See?"

"I don't take it as a sign."

"It's a sign that there's no use. Well, let's take aholt here. Let's show them different," said Patrick. It was about as strong as he ever got. All he wanted to do was shriek, Demons! Zombies! The dead!

The Indian was trying to restore the crease in his hat. "My chapeau," he said and laughed. "You should have written her more."

"I know," said Patrick.

"Drift in bad here in the winter?"

"Oh, yeah. We had some cattle trapped in the Moccasin draw one time and the bears raided into them, got 'em all. Bears just padded over that snow and started killing cows. Quite a wreck in there when it thawed. Looked like a Charlie Russell painting of the '86 blizzard, these half-gnawed skeletons up against the rocks . . ."

"Hunh."

"I have to throw up," said Patrick.

"If you're loud about it, crawl off away from the horses. I don't want to walk home."

Patrick got off a way, his hands deep in the lichen, and let it pour everywhere.

Catches continued in a louder voice: "My dad was a great one for throwing up on his horse and going on a blind-ass bronc ride into the cattle."

By the time Patrick found his way back, navigating by the white hat and the shapes of the horses when he couldn't find the hat, Catches was getting pretty choky. "See, she was what I had and she left me about thirteen different times and all this was, was the last time. And that's it. That's all she wrote. But she was crazy and I'm not. And sorta like you said, I won't be getting her back. All I'm going to say is this, and it might be the thing we fight over: She was more to me than she was to you."

Catches got out his knife. High above them, a heavy moon turned the scree brilliant as miles of quartz, and every so often something would come loose and roll, making a noise light, dry and clear as a single piece of bone.

"Do you deny what I said?" asked Catches.

Patrick followed the serration of forest, divided at the pass, and the vertical curve to the south of unearthly luminous granite.

"I don't deny it," said Patrick, absolutely letting something break in the name of some small, even miserable decency, something in its way perfect and unmissed by David Catches, who said, "Thank you."

The rest was the ride home.

28

BOTH PATRICK'S DESIRE FOR PRIVACY AND HIS MISTAKES IN human judgment sprang from the same vague feeling that things were very sad. This feeling had predated the death of his sister by some time. Still, he had not always felt this way. Now he did seem to always feel this way. And so he tried to stay on the ranch or make some blind attempt to get rid of the feeling that everything was sad-for-no-reason. The latter seemed to fail with absolute regularity; whereas staying on the ranch and working would just do. And he still thought Claire could change it all. Sometimes he felt that she had to. It made him uncomfortable.

Patrick got up suddenly, feeling he wasn't reacting appropriately to anything, that he wasn't doing any good. He heard the spring creak on the kitchen door and wondered who had come in. He shot the front of his shirt into his trousers with his hands, wobbled his head about and acted in general like someone trying to renew his concentration. This was getting to be a quieter house and the steps in the hallway, now plainly his grandfather's, were clear; but Patrick thought they were slow, and when the door opened, revealing Patrick standing in no particular place in the room and his grandfather exactly in the doorway with a newspaper, Patrick knew there was something not right. "Have you read this?" his grandfather asked, revealing little in his face to give away what was to be seen. Patrick started to read, then sat down. The newspaper had reported the funeral on the first page in unbelievable detail, including Patrick's rash remarks. The tone was unmistakably satirical and in the patented style of Deke Patwell. Basically it took the position that Patrick and Mary, long a local variety act, had pressed on amusingly after death.

"What did we do to them?" asked his grandfather. "I don't know."

"Patwell wrote that."

"Oh, I know."

"Where're you going, Pat?"

"To see Patwell."

"I think you better. I think this has to be fixed."

Strangely enough, nearly his first thought was, If they send me to jail, I'll never see Claire again. And finally, the almost infernal concentration of anger, the numb and almost stupid feeling in the front of the brain. His grandfather came down the front hall and gave Patrick a revolver.

"I don't want that," Patrick said.

"You ought to take something."

"I'm taking me, Grandpa."

"I think you ought to shoot the sonofabitch until you get tired of it."

"Well, I'm going to go down there and that's about all I know about it."

Patrick left the house and went to the barn and got an English blackthorn cane that had an ingenious ruler which slid out to measure the height of horses in hands.

The appointment desk lay in the eyeline of Patwell's open door, so that Patwell, sighting over the blue-washed Deadrock crone at the phone bank, could see Patrick had arrived. There were about ten reporters and secretaries in a large blond room without a view and a wilderness of baked-enamel office equipment in soothing gray. Patrick stared back at the faces and was refueled in his anger to know that these were the typists and copy editors and that they possessed a little glee that didn't belong to them.

Patwell called out, "What took you so long?"

Patrick just strolled around the receptionist into Patwell's office. He felt cold and peaceful.

"You want to close that door, Pat?"

"Not really, Deke. I just came by to find out why you wanted to talk about us in public like that."

"I run a newspaper and I thought you deserved it."

"Is that how it goes in editing? You give what you think people deserve?" He seemed to be helping Deke with his explanation.

"Yeah, that's pretty much how I feel. It's an old-fashioned newspaper."

"I feel you deserve that, you cuntful of cold piss," said Patrick, caning Patwell across the face. It took Patwell off his chair. "Get up," said Patrick. "Get back to your chair quickly. If I begin flailing your bottom with this thing, I'll lose my self-control." There was a livid mark across Patwell's face as he scuttled to his swivel chair. "Now," said Patrick, "that was meant to correct your attitude. You have hurt my feelings with your filthy fish-wrapper and you have hurt my grandfather, who is an old man. Do you follow me so far?" Patwell nodded hurriedly. Patrick wondered how many fingers in the outer office were dialing the police. "People just kind of live their lives, Deke. Y'know, they're not out there just as cannon fodder for boys with newspapers." Patwell nodded furiously. Patrick stared at him, feeling Patwell turn into an object again, one that had managed to besmirch his dead sister, and he could feel the crazy coursing of blood that he knew, unchecked, could turn him into a murderer. But then the police arrived, among them the chief of police, who demanded an explanation, and handled his gun.

"Deke wanted me to act out the Ronald Colman part from *The Prisoner of Zenda.* Isn't that so, Deke?"

The chief of police turned eyes of patented seriousness to the editor. "Do I arrest him?"

"No."

"Why?"

"Because he'll be put in jail."

"He's been before."

"When he gets out he'll kill me."

So something, after all, got through. Patrick just departed; when he passed through the large room with numerous brave-dialing employees, he said, "When this doesn't make tonight's newspaper, you'll know what kind of outfit you work for." They wrote that down, too; they were untouchable.

The cop caught up with him outside. "What else you have in mind for the day?"

"What's it to you?" Patrick asked, about a half-inch from the chief's face. It was turning into a Western.

"I don't know. You're still packing that cane and you aren't limping." The chief meshed both hands behind his head, thrusting forward an impervious abdomen.

"Don't let that throw you," said Patrick. Then he with-drew its inner slide. "See? You can measure your horse. This would be a Shetland pony and *this*—this would be Man o' War!"

"Well, thanks for the explanation, cousin."

"Anytime."

"I hope you don't need no help of any particular kind in the future."

Patrick smiled. "Not a chance. Not unless my car doesn't start or something. I might borrow your jumper cables."

The impact of Catches' love of Mary was driving him in circles. Even after Mary's death, it meant more than any-thing he had. Patrick was closest to it with Claire, and that was not very close.

❖ **29** ❖

AT ONE END OF THE GRANARY WAS AN OPEN SHED WITH BIG tools hanging on its walls, truck-sized lug wrenches, a scythe for the beggar's-lice that grew tall around the buildings and got into the horses' manes. There were also old irons for brands that the ranch owned, ones they quit using when they finally got a single-iron brand. There was a stout railroad vise, and Patrick's grandfather had been at it all morning, making a skinning knife out of a broken rasp.

"I'm going to kill me one more bugling bull, skin him with this and move to town."

"That's your plan, huh?" Patrick was kneeling on the ground, crimping copper rivets that had gone loose in the rigging of his pack saddles. That morning there had been a stinging fall breeze, and gear needed going through if he would make it to the hills before winter. "Got a spot picked out in town?"

"Those apartments across from the library."

"Sounds awful nice," said Patrick. "This has sure gotten to be a can of worms." Patrick wondered what he meant by that. The place wasn't at fault, but maybe something about it had begun to smell.

"That's what any ranch is, and this is a good one. It's got two hundred fifty miner's inches of first-right deeded water, plus a big flood right and the adjudication—y'know, if a guy cared to irrigate."

"I'll wait for some farmer to chase that water. My horses would rather be on prairie grass any day than wallowing around in alfalfa." They were starting in again.

"Well, I'll kill the one bull. Then look out town, here I come. After that, you can irrigate, not irrigate or piss up a rope."

"And you can be a star at the lending library."

"What?"

"Nothing."

Patrick worked away on the pack rigging, oiled the straps, coiled his lash ropes and canvas manties. It seemed crazy on a cool day, the two men polishing away on things they needed in order to get out, to go into the hills, to disappear. And yet Patrick didn't really want to disappear. All recent losses drove him to thinking of Claire. And he had no sense she did the same. Living on the ranch, which from his tank had seemed a series of bright ceremonies, was now more like entrapment in a motel on the interstate. Nor was he filled with a sense he could do something about it. It had stopped meaning anything.

❖ 30 ❖

CLAIRE CAME TO THE SIDE DOOR AT PATRICK'S KNOCK, AND HE was astonished to see how genuinely stricken she seemed. "Patrick, I haven't any idea what to say to you."

"It's all over. There isn't anything to say." Then he added, with ungodly bitterness, "The angels came and took her away."

He walked into the house and got his own coffee as though he lived there. Claire circled the kitchen in a preoccupied way, knocking cupboard doors shut. Patrick felt somehow choky when he looked over at her, so extraordinarily pretty in a yellow wash dress that seemed to belong to another time, like some unused memento of the dust bowl, something a girl driven off her bridal farm in Oklahoma and since gone on to old age in some anonymous California valley might have saved.

But the daughter of a desperate man of 1932 might well have worn such a yellow dress on a pretty day like today or worn it in hopes of seeing someone she loved. What if that turned out to be me? Well, a person could work at it. And then what? Then-what equals implications and I don't know what they are. I'm getting to know very damned little.

"When do you suppose Tio will come back?"

"It's a mystery."

"You still haven't talked to him?"

"No, and I've tried to. He showed up in Tulsa for a short time and now he's gone from there."

"Does this make you nervous?"

"*Yes.*"

"Me too. But I'm not sure why."

"If you knew Tio better, you'd know why."

"I would?"

"You certainly would."

The phone rang and Claire got up from the table in her yellow dress to answer it. She answered twice and put the phone down. "Whoever it was hung up," she said, trying not to let that seem significant.

Suddenly she grinned. "Can you press your weight?" she asked.

"No."

"I can. One fourteen." Patrick thought about a hundred and fourteen pounds in a yellow wash dress.

"Can you do the Cossack Drag?"

"I never tried."

"I did. I almost got killed."

They went up a stretch of white, chalky-looking road into a beautifully fenced pasture, almost a paddock; there were half a dozen old-time quarter mares with colts at their sides. Claire ran down their pedigrees; it was all front-of-the-book: King, Leo, Peppy, Rey del Rancho, Zantanon H and a granddaughter of Nobody's Friend. Patrick looked at them with their deep hips and shoulders, real cowman's horses of a kind that seemed to be vanishing, the kind that made you think of Shiloh, Cold Deck, Steel Dust, and Rondo, all legends of border fighting, match racing and the trail drives.

"Where did you find this set of mares?"

"Well, one by one, really. They were all scattered and neglected because they wouldn't raise running horses for Ruidoso. They're all old horses, and I bred every one of them to a last son of Poco Bueno, who's a three-legged fifty-dollar cripple in Alice, Texas, who belongs to a scrap-metal dealer. I figure those colts are a half-century old the day they're born. That chestnut mare is blind. Her foal will stand off by itself and be perfectly still just to tease her mother. Her mother will keep nickering because she can't locate her. Then that baby speeds up and nurses, and the crisis is over. —Why aren't you married?"

"Me?"

"Yes."

"Never came up."

"Have you had girl friends?"

"Oh sure, lots of those. But I didn't have a good picture of home life. I think that has kept me from settling down. Also, I can't get my own intentions straight. First I was a kid growing up. Then I was cowboying for a while, riding around in sedans from place to place with a saddle in the trunk. Then I was in school, out of school and in the Army. Now I'm on the ranch. I don't have an orderly approach. I don't see me with a Nobel prize or managing a Houston heart clinic."

"What about running your beautiful ranch?"

"Got my doubts there, too. I'd like to just see to the horses, but it ought to be farmed up quite a bit more. I always thought farming was a highly evolved form of mowing the lawn."

"It is."

The wind changed directions, gusting around the pasture, warm and piny, with the faint cool afterbreath of fall.

"Are you superstitious about things," Claire asked, "that have to do with life and death?"

"I haven't been so far."

"My grandmother lived with us in our old house near

Talalah. And one day the nails in the walls started falling out of their holes. That same day my grandmother died. There were nails all over the floor."

"I've never seen things like that. I don't believe my eyes are open to that sort of occurrence. Mary saw things like that. My experience with death was, it was real bluntlike and didn't send any calling cards." Suddenly gloom dashed in on him like some palpable dismal animal. They walked past the horse pasture with the deep-bellied mares grazing with their shadow colts, all the way to where the jack fence changed to steel-posted five-strand barbed-wire cattle fencing; and uphill of them, yearlings drifted along a hill to escape the flies in this new cool breeze.

The irrigation water came through a gap in the hillside like a bright tongue, and south of that a few hundred yards, they crossed into a piece of old meadow, full of original prairie flowers, all sweetly angled back toward the foothills by the prevailing wind, the same wind that swept Claire's yellow dress close around her long legs, the same dress that Patrick folded on the ground, the only thing that she had been wearing, so that she shivered and watched his gentle folding of the yellow cotton upon itself, then let him make love to her in something of the same way. Afterward, he glanced over and saw the one flat shoe, almost a slipper, she had crossed on the other, pinning a pale scarf in the light ground breeze, and with death and superstition and signs one could not read temporarily at bay, he felt a sweeping ache that in a child would have been the prelude to tears.

He said, "Leave everything and come with me." He was the one with the conviction. It scared her for a moment.

Immediately it struck Patrick that this attempt to spark his intentions across a gap not yet measured would never succeed. Nor was Claire shocked. Maybe she could have said the thing herself. Properly speaking, neither of them thought so. But Patrick felt like a sap—not a sap like the gland puppets of sudden love, the first-sighters and the stars of the one-night stands; but a sap of the heart, the amorous equivalent of someone who throws his clubs during a golf tournament.

"It should never have gotten this far."

"Why?" he asked.

"Because it's just to where it maybe could be extremely shattering. Besides it's . . . everything is . . ."

"What? Everything is what?"

"More than just coming home from the Army."

"No, it's not," said Patrick. "Everything *is* coming home from the Army."

"Okay, let's break it up. Boys, I want you to come out clean and punching."

"Don't be sarcastic."

"Well, we're down to that."

Suddenly there were details, tree trunks to bump into, rocks to trip over. In a Norway spruce next to the door, an old strand of Christmas lights deteriorated.

"I wish it could be like in books," said Patrick. "I wish it could be a big simp love story."

"I don't want to be in a big simp love story."

"My job would be to save the ranch."

"You're thinking of Gary Cooper."

"I guess there's a difference."

"A big difference. Gary Cooper saved the ranch. He had simp romances, too. Gary Cooper had his in barns. Book romances often take place in Europe. Cafés instead of barns. Me and Tio been to Europe. He brought his own ketchup and Pepto-Bismol. It was a gourmet tour."

"Sounds like quite a guy."

"He is," she said plainly.

"Well, I don't want to hear about him."

Inevitably Patrick drove home listening to a professional reminiscer on the radio who did Western topics twice a week:

"The awesome force of men and animals belittles all the images etched into the retinal filmstrips of my mind . . . The arena dust! . . . Churning hoof sounds . . . a truckload of hogs! Magnifique!"

31

PATRICK WAS BACK THE NEXT DAY. HE WAS LOSING IT. IT WAS late afternoon and their throats ached. He thought that there was fire in the daylight.

"We could fall in love," said Patrick, sickeningly swept past all reason.

"And then he'll hire a detective."

"What?" From the trance.

"Have you been listening?" She flicked a fox-spur from his hair. "We pull this and it's 'Katy, Bar the Door.' "

"What?" Where was he?

"Put on your boots. If we can keep walking, I won't feel so nervous. My God, what is this we're doing?"

Down toward the stream that swept past the fine old house, the heavy-trunked cottonwoods seemed to hold their dismaying branchloads of greenery in the awkward and beautiful whiteness which at a distance gives the valley river bottoms of the West almost their only sentimental quality. The rest consisted of towns with the usual franchise foreshore at either end; or in the case of Deadrock, the whirring elevations of the interstate, quiet only

when the arctic storms of middle winter feathered every
concrete radius with snow. Patrick felt drunk. The house
hung over him. Claire pulled herself against him in the
warm air. He panicked at the driveway. There might have
been too many cars. There might have been chartered
aircraft or police. There might have been dead people or
banshees to militate against this surge that held him in its
force.

They were in a bed in a room with a south-facing window that the sun crossed like a bullet. When the horses
whinnied to be fed at the end of the day, gathered below
the darkening window in a plank corral, Claire's tears
chilled all over Patrick's face. The old dive-bomber comic
they found in the trunk was crumpled under the pillows.
A pale star had bravely arisen to follow the sun across the
window; brave, thought Patrick, because it privately
knew it was two hundred thousand times the size of our
solar system, though its millennial flames are the only
thing that would stop me now. All it is, is this small evening star. The horses are hungry. We are sore. Saying she
loved me made her cry. In the iron-cloistered control station of the fast American tank was the glossy photograph
of a German princess's strangely expressive anus, and beside that the release buttons for the rockets. The whir of
treads on deep Teutonic sod brought peculiar memories.
Marion Easterly, the mystery heartthrob, the archangelic
semaphor known as the Dead Father and now the snowy
grid beneath which his sister would lie forever were all
contained in that upendable shallow bowl, the rim of
which divided past and future. I am finally outside the
bowl.

32

PATRICK DROVE HOME IN THE NIGHT. THE YARD LIGHTS WERE strong in the blackness of the valley's gradual elevation southward like the scrambled approach to a bridge. After he had said to Claire, Leave everything and come with me, she had asked, Where? And at first he had been hurt, searching, as men do, for blind love, but then, even to his credit, he did indeed wonder where they could go and it became clear that he still, as of the Army, hadn't exactly returned to the ranch and they might just as well go there; and that that in turn might give him the handle he had long sought on his situation there, might carry him back to the sense of purpose his great-grandfather had had upon his return from Aguinaldo's Native Insurrection, the dynamite firecrackers on the Fourth of July and the general feeling of being able to see farther than your nose in front of you. He nearly strangled on his last idea, as though Claire should provide this firelight; he felt ashamed. There was a porcupine waddling across his turn-off; he stopped the truck, stared at its awkward purpose and wondered if the porcupine had anyplace to go. Patrick ached. He thought, literally, that he was aching like a fool. Chest pains. Incapable-of-judgment. The best thing would be for us to move to the ranch together. Nevertheless, he imagined the center of his mind looked like an asshole taped on the dashboard of the tank.

He walked into the dark kitchen and turned the light on over the stove ventilator. He made himself a drink. He didn't know what time it was and he felt guilt but could not pin it down. He would rather have felt the guilt than the sadness-for-no-reason. The latter was a ball breaker, whereas guilt was easily anesthetized with not all that much bourbon. Then the phone rang and of course it was Tio.

"Tio, where are you?"

"Cain't let on, Pat. *Where are you?*"

"Right where you called me. In my kitchen."

"Well, I was just settin here wonderin if anybody there in Montana had got so eat up with the dumb ass they life was endangered."

"I can't see that they could be."

"How's my stud colt?"

"He's rank and squeally. He's going to make a great gelding."

"Well, Fitzpatrick, I'm down here shootin quail and thinkin about things. We got good dogs and a bunch of Mexicans to shag dead birds. It's the life, but they practically raise snakes and you can't get through that blackjack and cat's-claw with a horse. So you're down among them. You're down among the snakes, Fitzpatrick. You follow me?"

"Yes, I do." Patrick tilted his glass until he no longer saw movement among the ice cubes. He was getting nervous.

"I suppose I shouldn't be leavin Claire to fend like that. Most generally a man's a fool to leave one that Cadillacky to its own devices."

"How did you get down there, anyway, Tio?"

"In a Bell helicopter with full avionics and a walnut interior. Had to fly around all them bullshit mountains up there to get to a place fit for human habitation. I knew that colt was dumber than Fido's Ass, but I want you to turn him back to me double tough. I expect that. And if

Claire's lonely, call her and give her that Dial-a-Better-Day exchange in Deadrock; I'll be back when I get back."

"Okay."

"Fitzpatrick, life is a shit sandwich and I take a bite every day. You do too. But if you had to eat it in one swallow, you'd choke on it and die a very unpleasant death." He rang off and that was that.

Patrick stood still and then trickled whiskey down the inside of his glass like a chemist in a high school play performing an experiment; and in fact the glazed look on his face did seem very much like bad acting. " '*Okay,*' " he said aloud. "Why did I say okay? That Oklahoman shit-heel suggested that I give Claire the Dial-a-Better-Day number. And I said okay!" But he looked up Dial-a-Prayer in the directory and made the call. With God, it turned out, every loss is a gain. Hello. Thank you for calling Dial-a-Better-Day. Disruption and sadness will be banished. I wonder if they're thinking about that sadness stalking me, that evil ferret sadness that ingests five times its weight each day. Hearts will be healed and God will lift us up. Garlands instead of ashes. Sixty-first chapter of Isaiah. God will see you in the next reel. He is Our Projectionist. I will wring His Little Neck if I get another instance of sadness-for-no-reason.

"Darling?"

"Yes."

"It's me."

"I know it is. Oh God."

"What are you doing?"

"I'm in bed. I'm here, scared of the dark."

"Should I come over?"

"I don't think so."

"Guess what."

"What?"

"Guess."

"Tio called," said Claire. Panic was in her voice.

"How did you know?"

"It was easy. Where is he?"

"He wouldn't say. He was quail hunting. All he'd say was that life was a shit sandwich and we had to take a bite every day."

"He was being very intimate with you. Normally he saves the sandwich speech until much deeper into the situation."

"What do you mean by that?" Patrick demanded, thinking this had happened before.

"I mean like in an oil deal or something. By the time they've cased the well, fractured and done their logging —y'know, kind of late in the game—he tells some newcomer in the business up north here in the Overthrust or something that life is a shit sandwich etcetera. Just when the guy is hanging on by his teeth. So he is either being intimate with you or he thinks you're hanging on by your teeth."

"I think I'm following."

"Did he menace you?"

"I'm not sure."

"How not sure?"

"Well, he said that if you had to eat the sandwich in one bite, you'd choke to death."

"He was menacing you."

❖ 33 ❖

PATRICK LAY IN BED AND STARED AROUND AT THE FURNISH-
ings of his room. There was only one lamp and, overhead,
a moth-filled milk-glass ceiling fixture that gave off an
awful light. The bedside lamp was a real must. How many
things, he wondered, shall we call real musts? What about
ball bearings? A real must in defending one's self against
the natives was a handful of stout ball bearings. The 2nd
Division went up against Villa with only their uniforms
and their ball bearings; without a belief in The Maker, a
real must, all there would have been to show would have
been the ball bearings, while Villa took his false gods to
Deauville for the races. Jesus Christ, he thought, let us
turn our thoughts to Claire; the mind is no boomerang.
Throw it far enough and it won't come back.

Did Tio in fact smell a rat, or only a quail? Was Patrick
the Montana version of the Tulsa hidey-hole, where ole
Shit proved bulletproof? He felt ashamed of having had
this thought. Shamed and chilled. Himself as part of a test
of sexual allegiance. Maybe he meant to out-Tio Tio, to
get just hopelessly Western about this situation, this fix, to
see who, just *who*, was the standup gunslinger of the two.
It is typical of me, he thought, to foresee a major show-
down well before an acquaintanceship has been struck
between the principals. Am I not rude? I am.

He hadn't been rude yet, but he would have to cut back
on his drinking or it was going to all burst forth in a
clenched and dangerous teetering toward love, requited

or otherwise. This was the sort of isolated dam break that
Patrick was susceptible to. When he could identify it, he
thought it was ridiculous. He didn't see anything now at
all and he was therefore wide open to any repetitious mis-
take, precisely at a time in his life when he could least
stand repetition. But then, where was the repetition; and
couldn't this just be a fear, as guilt is a fear, of something
that didn't exist?

He drifted away. One of the first lines he ever learned
from a song was, "I got a hot-rod Ford and a two-dollar
bill." He was hitchhiking from Two Dot and he heard it in
the back seat of a hot-rod Ford. He had never seen a two-
dollar bill. Up front an older boy necked with his girl.
Patrick could smell something . . . well, something. He
had not imagined that there would be anything to smell.
He tried not to stare or draw breath through his nose.
Breath through his nose, he knew, would be a mortal sin.
He looked instead at the sagebrush flats and streaks of
water running from spring-flooded culverts in the creek
bottoms.

"How far you going?"

"What?" Seal off that nose, she's wriggling.

"Where you getting off at?"

"Deadrock."

"We ain't going to Deadrock. I'm shutting down this
side of Harlowton–– You ever seen a rubber?"

"Yeah." He hadn't. He was mouth-breathing and gaping
into the sagebrush.

"Ever seen one like this?" It was a Ted Williams brand
and it had the ball player on the label, ready to pound
one out of Fenway Park.

"No, I sure haven't."

"Came out of a machine," said the girl. "In Great Falls

because of the air base. It's a year and a half old. It's give out and it's still in the wrapper. That's about how I was raised, buddy."

"Up around them bases," said the driver, "a rubber don't have a long life to look forward to."

"It does in Harlowton," said the girl doggedly.

"I ought to rape your ass!"

"You and what army?"

The driver went into the hot-rod slump, left hand fingering the wind vane, upper body wedged between the wheel and the door. It worked; she crawled on over and Patrick craned at the landscape, wondering if this was going to end up in confession, then finally filling his lungs with the immemorial musk that fogged the interior of that hot-rod Ford, thinking: Purgatory at the very least.

He would have to go back to that, just to find one level of the power Claire had come to have for him. At the very minimum she was the lost ghost of the gold dredge.

❖ 34 ❖

TODAY WAS GOING TO REQUIRE A DEPARTURE, A MIGHTY DEparture, from the recent pattern of thinking, drinking, funeral attending, cooking, baby-sitting his grandfather, caning editors and tampering with love. Because the ranch was falling apart. It was somehow terrific to rediscover that the ranch was not a dead, immutable thing. He could see from the upper road where one headgate had washed out, and there was a great mean scar where the water had gouged at the pretty hillside, and the topsoil from that particular part of the ranch was now in the

Yellowstone River on its way to North Dakota. That had to be fixed. There were four places where the wire was down on the west-division fence; that would have to be pulled up and restapled. Things were a mess and he was getting excited. He was going to need his fence stretcher and fencing gloves and it was still going to be tops in mindless. But if he had any luck at all, this was going to last for years. It was like the heart trouble he wished for and never got.

He started hurting about halfway through the day. He hauled salt and mineral blocks, ponying a second horse up to the forest line. Then gathered thirty black yearlings from the brush along the creek where the flies had driven them from their feed. He gathered them into one end of the corral and he penned them off with a steel panel. He hung the heavy spray canister from a canvas strap over the sore muscles of his shoulders and waded among the fly-swarming backs, pumping with one hand and directing the nozzled wand with the other. When he was nearly done, one white-eyed steer flicked out a rear hoof and kneecapped Patrick, and he had to go sit down until the pain subsided and the knee swelled up tight within his jeans. He sat on the dirt of the corral, the canister still in place, tapped one dirty boot with the spray wand, looked through the steel panel at the milling steers as they felt the flies' liftoff; like them, he rolled fool eyes to heaven and thought: Claire, my knee hurts.

He hung the sprayer on a corral post and rode back down to the ranch. He was so tired that when he unsaddled the horse, he just drop-kicked the saddle out of his way and threw the bridle in a heap. He grained the horse and kept her down for the next day and went inside.

Then, while he was making dinner for his grandfather, who was sorting a shoe box of assorted cartridges, he noticed through the kitchen window that everything was covered with a thin layer of dust.

"Did the wind blow real hard here today?"

"No."

"How come everything is covered with dust?"

"A helicopter landed in the yard."

"*What?*"

"Helicopter."

"Who was in it?"

"Nobody got out. Here's an old Army Springfield round."

"How long did it stay there?"

"Oh, bout an hour. Made quite a racket. They never shut that big propeller off. I really didn't want to walk near it." Tio had made an aerial visit under power and Patrick had missed it: a lost effect, like rabbits jumping from a top hat in an empty room.

Patrick had given up on his cooking since his grandfather had gone off his specialties. So now he made dopy chicken casseroles or things he could cook all day in a crock; and today he had prepared, of all things, a big bowl of red Jell-O to set beside the aerosol can of Reddi-Wip; and it was in its tremulous surface that he first detected the return of the helicopter, a faint sound, a drumming, like one's pulse; then rapidly magnifying as it moved toward them. Its horizontal motion could be felt to stop, and high above the house the waves of sound centered.

Patrick walked out the front door and could see the great insect shape high above the ranch. It made him nervous. The moment he stepped into the yard, the helicopter began to move toward the mountains, disappearing finally through a narrow pass. Patrick went back inside and thumbed open *The Joy of Cooking*.

"I wish that movie hadn't gone away," said his grandfather. "Maybe there was movie people in that helicopter."

"I doubt it."

"They could have been scouting locations."

"I suppose."

"Everybody loves a Western."

"How do you know it was a Western?"

"*Hondo's Last Move*? What else could it be?"

"The word around here was it was about a child molester named Hondo."

"I didn't know that. God, I didn't know *that*."

"Can you eat chicken and dumplings again?"

"Sure. Can we go to the movies?"

"I'm pretty tired, Grampa."

"Or there's one with Greer Garson on TV. It's about a factory, I think."

"Maybe that would be better. Besides it'll be late once these dishes are cleaned up."

"I'll help."

"Okay."

"Tomorrow can we look at apartments?"

"Sure."

"I can't remember which rifle this went to," said his grandfather in disgust, placing the cartridge next to the Jell-O. "I think it was that one that the horse fell with coming out of Falls Creek with Arnie."

"I didn't know Arnie, Gramp." Patrick was sick of these unreferenced tours of memory. Fucking Arnie, anyway.

"He was the scissorbill from up around Plentywood. I don't know. Anyway, I know it's gone."

"You want a drink?"

"No. That was a funny-looking machine, that helicopter. Shame Mary couldn't have seen it. I didn't have my hat and my hair was blowing all over. I got dirt in my nose. It went straight up and I lost it in the sun. It was exactly like the movies. Maybe it was full of prisoners and there's this guy who didn't shave, with a tommy gun."

Patrick was getting depressed as he cooked. Tio, he guessed, was home. He literally pined for Claire and there wasn't anything he could think to do about it. And there was something about his grandfather's running on, which didn't usually bother him, that was getting at his nerves. Still, he could fall back on the day's work, a new regime toward bringing the ranch back to order. There was some warm memory tugging at him that he couldn't quite isolate; and as he cooked, he searched his mind for it, feeling that it would cheer him up. Then it came: It was the velvet hydraulic rush of his tank over Germany, the orderly positions of the crew, and being the captain.

"Fitzpatrick."

"Hey, Tio."

"Awfully sorry about your sister."

"Thanks for saying so."

"And remember, it was her right to do that. She's the only one to know if it was a good idea. It can be just the thing; I'm persuaded of that."

"Okay."

"Say, how much do you want for your ranch?"

"It's not for sale, Tio."

"I just went down and dumped that Cat-Track joint that was such a thorn in our sides, that quicksand trap on the north Canadian, and the money's burning a *hole* in my pocket."

"This is my grandfather's and my home."

"Well, move ass to town. I want to spend this *dinero*. The old man tell you I came and looked at the place?"

"Were you in a helicopter?"

"That was me. That you come out in the yard at suppertime?"

"Yup."

"I thought so. Say, are you sleeping with my wife?"

Not a word in reply.

"Leafy, am I not thoughtless? I am. Left you in a cold corral with no kisses. Here is a kiss. What a beautiful horse you are." Leafy exhaled and changed weight on her feet. It seemed so extraordinary to Patrick that this watermarked mare with eyes like tide pools could also be twelve hundred pounds of orchestral muscle, could trust and work for you, could ride the continually moving hands of the mortal clock with you, could take you in the hills, help you win a rodeo or work cattle, could send you gliding with new tallness on a part of the earth that was worth all the trouble. "What do you know of trouble, Leafy? Or do you take the position that it is my department?"

Onward to the restoration of order: mucking stalls, wheelbarrowing the manure across the road onto the rich pile that would be so useful to a determined gardener with a nice ass. Then he went up on the metal roof of the granary before it got too hot and tarred over the nail holes as he had to each year. He had put the roof on and had nailed in the troughs of the corrugation instead of the lands, as one is supposed to, and so it had to be tarred yearly. He was determined to ride Leafy today because he thought he glimpsed sadness-for-no-reason in her eyes.

When Leafy was born, her mother dropped her in the last piece of snow in a spring pasture. Patrick found the foal, a clear, veinous membrane around her shoulders, shivering in the snow, her seashell hooves just beginning to harden in the air. He put an arm under her butt and one under her neck and lifted her out onto the warming prairie grass while the mother nickered in concern. Then he drew the membrane down off her body and let the mare lick her dry. The watermarks in her coat were like leaves and Patrick named her while the mare contracted and drove out the afterbirth; Patrick lifted the placenta, shaped like the bottom of a pair of long underwear with one short leg, and scrutinized it for completeness; a missing piece retained in the mare could be fatal. Leafy wobbled to her feet after pitching over a few times and stood, straight-legged, springy-pasterned, with her exaggerated encapsulated knees. Patrick put iodine on her navel stump, which made her leap. The mother stood and Leafy ducked under to nurse. The mare kept lifting a rear leg from the pain of new milk; then the two, big and little shadows, glided away to their life together. Patrick went off through the orchard; and by the time he had started down the hill to the house, he could hear the birds arguing in the afterbirth. In his mind he had marked the foal for himself.

"At least can we look for apartments tomorrow?"

"I promise. I'm just tired, Grampa. Besides, you want to see them in the light."

"They have lights, Pat. They have electricity, for crying out loud. They're about two blocks from the movies."

"Still, you want the outside to be nice. You want to look around."

"If I was worried how they looked on the outside, I'd stay on the ranch."

"I don't know what this bee in your bonnet is, anyway. Why *aren't* you staying on the ranch?"

"Because I see things I can't do anymore, and in an apartment I won't. I won't have to watch you do things worse than I did them. I'll be protected from such a sight." Patrick was angered this time by his grandfather. But even irritated, he dreaded seeing the apartments.

❖ 35 ❖

THE LIGHTS WHEELED AGAINST THE HOUSE AND STOPPED. Then Patrick could see only the darkness. But when the car door opened after quite a long moment and its interior lights went on, he saw that it was Claire. He raced down the stairs to the front door. He turned on the hall light and stepped outside. When she got to the door, Patrick felt the ardent flush of blood through his chest.

He said, "I had a sore knee," then held her and kissed her. She seemed limp or exhausted.

"You what?"

"I wanted to tell you yesterday I had a sore knee. You weren't here. It's not sore anymore, but I wanted to be a baby about it."

Claire followed Patrick through the doorway, past ten year's history of overshoes, overshoes with lost buckles, overshoes covered with the manure of cattle long since vanished through takeout windows, and overshoes of drunks who failed to return. They sat in the kitchen and

Patrick found her request for whiskey an inspiration; so now the cheerful label of George Dickel's bourbon was between them, and if it had not been for Claire's strangely stricken look, all would have been not just happy but beyond belief. It was the middle of the night and they were alone together on Patrick's ranch. He knew there was something going on; but he was determined to turn things into his first impression no matter what.

"He's home."

"I know. I talked to him."

"Well, I don't know what his problem is."

"What's he doing?"

"He's just kind of raging around. He sent his pilot into town. First he was going to sleep in the helicopter. I kept saying what's the matter, and he says it's boring. I'm bored. I said I was sorry. When he goes down there and they get on those phones, a lot of them start using pills and they get very cross. But this time I don't know. He used to be so sweet. I think he must know something. Then he came inside and said we were going to forget it; but first he just wanted to know what in the hell I had achieved in his absence. I said nothing and he said he didn't think so. Well, we even got over *that*, which maybe was too bad"—she refilled her drink one-handed, leaning on the other, the pale thick braid coming over her shoulder across her pretty breasts—"because when we went upstairs, he grew extremely nasty with me."

Patrick's stomach twisted. "How?"

"Never mind. It was simply too coarse for words. It was nasty." She took a long breath. "So what I told him was he had the wrong person. He needed someone you just pay, because he sort of saw it as I was to do as I was told. So Tio yells, 'Are you talking about a whore? Fine! I'd like three!' He said that I was a whore in every way except the one that counted. So that's where I am."

"Where?"

"Trying to find three whores for Tio!"

"Are you serious?"

"Absolutely. And I told him so." She smiled weakly. "I was hoping you'd know where I could find them."

"Is he safe?"

"Oh sure. It's just that he can get right repulsive with me. He'll treat them like queens and overpay, too—"

"Are you calling his bluff?" Patrick felt as though he'd fallen in the middle of a dispute wherein he feared discovering some passion. This had some of the signs of revenge and he was not entirely happy to help.

"I'll help," he said.

So instead of being alone together on the ranch with the dwarf owls drifting across the yard through the yard light, the coyotes trickling down out of the hills toward dawn when the cool inversion changed the smell from cottonwood to evergreen, instead of that, they were barreling through the night toward a Deadrock cathouse. At least, thought Patrick, we are in her car and I'm damn well going to insist on a ride home. Purgatory at the very least.

Once again—that is, not since he had first come home and sought rumors of Mary and had overcome his resistance to the facts—once again, this time with Claire, he crossed the footbridge over the clear-running ditch and knocked on the whorehouse door. He remembered the television debate as to the fetus's right to life, the coffee cans naming the girls, the kitchen timers. The door opened and

David Catches greeted Patrick and Claire. Patrick introduced Claire to David and they went in.

"What are you doing here, David?"

"What are you doing here?"

"I can't give you the instant replay. The story's a little hard to tell."

They passed into the living room; the television was on and girls were scattered in teasing fragmentary bits of clothing. Loretta, the former homecoming queen, wearing almost nothing, gave Patrick the kiss of a very old friend; but still he felt something tighten in his crotch. There were somewhat brutal sounds continuously to be heard in neighboring rooms; and Patrick thought, This wonderful spot is good for our town! Loretta's playfulness had taken some of the sting from his situation.

"I met Mary here," said David. "I guess I came back, y'know . . . old times. Anyway, I make sure everything is okay. In other words, I got a job."

Suddenly a door opened and a very happy, inebriated man of fifty pirouetted into the room. He was naked and tumescent and he had spotted Claire. "Where were you when I ordered?" he demanded to know.

"She doesn't work here," David said politely.

"Someone's trying to hog her," he said. "I'm gd cstmr and I won't stnd fr it."

"She's with the police," said David. Patrick couldn't take his eyes off Loretta, and the shadowy, lounging figures watching television were getting under his skin.

"That's just great," said the drunk. "Now I've lost my hard-on. Where my shoes?" He stumbled disconsolately toward the door he'd emerged from. "Where'm I gone get nother? Can't get nother. Only hard-on I had. But who cares? None of you care . . . " He drifted away. "You're all women's libbers," he added.

Once the situation had been explained to David, whom the girls called Cochise, and a cash settlement made by Claire, they were ready to head for Tio Burnett's ranch. "Let's get a head count here!" David called as the three girls pulled on revealing one-piece quick-draw dresses. Claire noticed Patrick staring. She was very slightly and most delicately irate.

"You think they're pretty, don't you?" she said very close to his face. His heart soared.

"Well, they *are* pretty."

"I thought the best things in life were free."

"This is the major exception."

Patrick, Claire, Loretta, Deirdre and Tana went out through the door, Patrick shaking hands once more with Catches, considering that friendship was somewhere possible, and in the mixture of perfume, mysterious sounds behind doors, weak drinks and TV, he thought he had seen Mary's ghost for the first time in a form he didn't believe would kill him.

Claire gave the girls a wide and too-sunny smile, the lightest crow's feet at the corners of her slate eyes, and said to the women, "Get on in." The three climbed into the backseat; Claire got in and Patrick prepared to drive. No amount of air-conditioning could daunt the garden of scents that filled the interior of the car. Patrick felt thrilled.

"Where exactly we going, Pat?" Loretta asked.

"Remember the old Leola Swenson place in the Crazies?"

"Yeah."

"Well, there."

"You two know each other?" Claire asked.

"Yes."

They headed up north on Main Street. The brick false fronts, the glitter of the bars and keno parlors, the sight of the grand old stone railroad station's arcades lit only by passing cars, seemed to make things extraordinarily cheerful. Patrick could hear the polishing of silk stockings on shifting legs in back, and it occurred to him that he hardly knew anyone who wore them anymore; they were worn to be removed.

"Is this a Cadillac?" Deirdre asked.

"Yes," said Claire.

"I was going to get one. Montana has such tough usury laws you can make great deals with General Motors' financing plans. But I wanted front-wheel drive. So I got a Toronado."

Tana said, "I'll never pass the driver's test. I can*not* parallel park."

"That's because you refuse to pull up even with the car in front of you. That is absolutely the only way it will work," Loretta said.

"It gives me the creeps to pull up that far. I keep thinking someone will get my spot."

"They get your spot anyway, because *you* never get it."

"Who is this person we're going to see?" Loretta asked.

"My husband," said Claire. The car was silent. Shapes passed the window in that silence: sawdust burners glowing in the night, various spots of lights on the remote hills like beacons, patterned somehow, as though they were to be read from space.

Deirdre piped up innocently, "You sure are understanding!"

"Thank you," said Claire grimly.

"Will there be any rough stuff?" Loretta inquired.

"No."

"Good. I sure wouldn't want to cross that sagebrush in the dark."

Tana asked, "Will you be with us, Claire?"

"I'm sorry, no," said Claire. This was really getting appalling to her. The impulse, it seemed to Patrick, had long since disappeared into the gritty logistics.

"I think, ladies," Patrick said, "that it would be best, all things considered, if nobody saw me tonight."

"Mum's the word."

When they got to the bottom of the road, Patrick turned off the lights and crept toward the house. There were low brushy willows at one side of the road, and they glowed in the moonlight with an extraordinary pallor. The darkness, the glow of the instruments, the invisible female presences, made Patrick think of the Army. Or the inside of aircraft. It seemed to him that Claire was sitting extremely upright and that that was somehow distinct from the warm, crowded people in back. She was lit by instruments.

"You'll have to walk from here," said Patrick. "Just to be safe." The house, emerged from the elevation to the road, was completely lit from within; but nothing other than windows were illuminated, a crazily assorted series of panels in the darkness itself. It looked unfinished, like a sketch for something unearthly. Nobody crossed one of the panels; it was a terrifically detailed emptiness.

"I'll pick you up in three hours, ladies," said Claire.

"Here?"

"No, I'll drive up."

They watched the women walking toward the lights until they were absolutely perfect silhouettes, moving like three black flames to the house.

Patrick turned the car around and started downhill.

When he had gone far enough, he turned the lights on and glanced over at Claire. Her face was shining with tears. For three hours, they were on their own, the thud of freedom. Patrick thought of, and rejected, numerous simple questions before he spoke. Then he asked, "Why did you marry him?" She turned quickly to look at Patrick.

"Because I loved him," she said; she was angry.

At the bottom of the hill, you could turn north or south on the pavement, or west toward the Bridger on the county road. "Boy, this is a quiet car," Patrick said, then stopped to think. He turned left to get closer to his ranch and to calm his nerves. They were nearly to Deadrock, circling slowly above the lights on the interstate, before Claire spoke: "Will we wake anybody up if we go back to your place?"

"No."

"It will be quiet there?"

"Could be a little too quiet."

The interstate kept curving into them, fanning the lights of Deadrock farther and farther northward. The trucks eastbound in the night mounted from the valley and rolled with a peculiarly fatal motion until they were out of sight.

They made love in Patrick's bedroom. They had simply not spoken. There had been a temptation to leave the motor running. Claire's breath shuddered and she held on to Patrick rather than held him. He was overcome with a blind tenderness. They each smelled like the women in the car. He held her hips and turned his forehead into her fragant neck and felt his own throat ache pointlessly. Suddenly it was out of their control, like a movie film that has come off its sprockets, leaving vivid incomprehensible images. Then stops, awaiting repair.

"Can you breathe?"

"Yes."

"Like this?"

"Yes, I can breathe fine."

"Sun'll be up in three hours."

"I know it."

"But you'll still be driving in the dark."

There was a very long spell of silence.

"I'll be driving home from here in the dark." Then she burst into convulsively merry laughter. "The sun should be up by the time I get back from dropping the ladies — *Oh God!*"

Patrick burned, watching her dress. There were things Claire did, not entirely necessary to the simple restoration of her clothes. The braid lay in the channel of her back. She leaned to kiss him good night before she had covered her breasts. Her eyes had now a velocity, an intention and loss of weakness that made him know that although their time was gone, she wanted him again.

"Amo shuffle on home."

"I think you should."

"Natty don't work for no CIA."

"That's clear."

"I have chores."

"Right . . ."

"No car pool up that way. Babylon by Cadillac."

"Seems like a shame."

"What?"

"Hit and run. Nothing eventual."

She said, "It's what we have."

36

IN THE THREE HOURS PATRICK SLEPT, A FOOT OF SNOW FELL. It must have fallen on an almost windless night, because where it cleaved at roof's edge the angle was perfect and vertical. Some of it fell in powdery sheets onto the still-green lilacs. But the world was white as Christmas, and the Absarokas beyond seemed a subtle interstitial variant of that same whiteness, a photograph with two or three planes of focus. The first thing that Patrick heard was a rifle booming into silence; and when he went to the window in his drawers, he could see down into the yard, where his grandfather, head shrouded under an immemorially weathered John B. Stetson hat, was sighting in his old Winchester. He had dragged a table into the yard and was firing toward the elevation of earth beneath the orchard. Patrick took down the binoculars from on top of his dresser to see what he was firing at: an old Hills Brothers can, with the man in the yellow caftan drinking coffee, wedged in the bank. As Patrick watched, the caftan disappeared, round after thundering round, until only the head and fez remained; then in one resonant crack that rolled down the creek bottom, they were gone too. The old man restacked the empties in their box, removed five live rounds, put those in his shirt pocket and stood up on the one good leg and the one slightly crooked, mule-kicked leg that had nearly got him into movies.

By God, thought Patrick, the bastard can still shoot.

Once Patrick got downstairs, he could smell Hoppe's number 9 powder solvent, one of the most sentimental

fragrances in the land. Before he turned the corner into
the kitchen, he could make out the muscles in the old
man's forearm as he raced the cleaning rod in and out of
the barrel; he stopped and watched the patches accumu-
late from gray-black to white, heard the minute am-
phibian sound of the oilcan and the swish of cloth. Then
when he heard the rifle stand in the corner with a solid
thud, he imagined it would be safe to reveal himself without making any promises about hunting trips.

"Good morning."

"Good morning, Pat."

"That you shooting?"

"Yes. The old smokepole will still drive a tack."

"What were you shooting at?"

"I was shooting a little tin. I shot it till I got tired of it.
Then I quit."

"I suppose you want to go hunting."

"No, I don't. I want to look at apartments. You take me.
I can't be arguing with landlords. I'm the ramrod of the
Heart Bar."

Arnoldcrest Apartments was built in the twenties and,
architecturally, made more than a passing bow to the
phantom district known as Constantinople. There was
something secretive about its ground plan, a suggestion of
courtyards and fountains that never materialized from the
beginning, arched entryways and recessed windows—all
once the hope of a man dreaming of the deserts of the
East, but quite another thing to the widows and pension-
ers of the Northwest, flattened by snow, fixed incomes and
a hundred thousand newspapers. On the other hand, one
could hang out an upstairs window, perhaps a little peri-
lous for the octogenarians, and see nine Montana bars.

That was not all bad. They could be reached in five minutes at a walk, three at a trot, round-trip times to the contrary notwithstanding.

They walked from the parked truck. Patrick thought, It's Istanbul, not Constantinople. Why did Constantinople get the works? That's nobody's business but the Turks'. This is what the yellow man in the fez was trying to tell me: We've got everything here but the harem.

Mr. Meacham, the manager, had been in the merchant marine and wore his khakis and T-shirt and crew cut with the same directness of statement—washing versus pressing, cleanness versus grooming—that Patrick imagined had been the measure of the man on the high seas. He had two further thoughts in a row: One, is this how you dress if it is a regular part of your job to take Arnoldcrest clients out the door feet first? Two, is this how you dress to set up a disciplinary contrast with old cowboys and ranchers who do not maintain up-to-date standards of personal hygiene? In other words, does Mr. Meacham batter a door down with his crew cut when he suspects bed wetting? This was a little like packing lunch for Junior's first school day. Patrick was extremely nervous.

First they explored a one-bedroom. It had plaster walls and milled wainscoting that must have been done on a production line fifty years ago. The sockets were waist-high, and there was an overhead fixture in the livingroom with green glass cherubs. The steam registers bracketed the one decent-sized window, and the window gave onto a view of the Emperial Theater and the Hawk, a little bar that sold cheese and cigars.

"Who's living in the building?" asked the grandfather.

"A number of people like yourself," said Meacham. "Some terrific people. A number of former cowboys."

"Any Indians?"

"Yes, Mr. Stands-in-Timber is just down the corridor with his mother, who is said to be a very good cook. They speak sign language to themselves, and so they're very quiet neighbors indeed."

It *was* fairly quiet, though the lonesome sound of day-time television came from behind brass-numbered doors. Meacham stood at ease, awaiting a decision.

"We're a hop, skip and a jump from the hospital," he threw in. "Lots of folks feel there's something nice about that. It would take all day to list the churches. Some people like to worship with the radio, but me, I'm for getting out and doing it if you're able."

The two-bedroom looked vast, though it might have been its emptiness that made it seem so. It faced the back lots of small homes with children, high garbage output and racket, which made these vacant rooms seem sad to Patrick. He was afraid there would be too many remind-ers of the years now lost to his grandfather; though his grandfather might know the children weren't going to get anywhere, either. Nevertheless, he pressed for the one-room with the view of the theater. And he arranged for additional basement storage for guns, saddles and pan-niers.

"You have any girl friends, Mr. Fitzpatrick?"

"Don't be so goddamned stupid."

The snow had turned to slush in the street, and people passing the Arnoldcrest had their overcoats drawn around themselves in defense less against this one soggy day than against the five months of winter just now easing itself out of the Arctic. Patrick struck a bargain for his grandfa-ther's new home. He'd move in after elk hunting.

They stopped at the cemetery. It was Patrick's first visit, although, to his surprise, his grandfather had al-ready been, once to remove an ensemble of funeral decorations and once to see if the grass was going to get a start by winter. Patrick thought it was preposterous to view this as a "visit"; but seeking to calm down, he was increasingly bent on imitating the actions of ordinary civilians. The snow had covered the grave and that seemed somehow a friendly fact, a mantle over someone troubled in ways he had never been able to understand, unless it was just the sadness-for-no-reason. Near them an old woman in a heavy twill overcoat sorted flowers by their stems, turning three half-dead bunches into one pretty bouquet and one bundle of waste vegetation. She sternly planted the doomed flowers in snow over her grave, returned to an old Chevrolet she had left idling, and departed, throwing the flowers that hadn't made it into the backseat. She looked very practical in the flying snow; and Patrick thought there was something to be emulated in that, as to one's arrangements. Old people, he imagined, daily put their shoulders to a wheel that would break every bone in a young man's body.

But this cemetery was a strange place, a prime piece of land, with Views. And in all respects it was best seen as real estate. The land holdings were small, especially by the standards of the West. For some reason you had "plots" instead of "lots." It occurred to Patrick that as his home country cooked down into smaller and smaller pieces, "plots" were going to be the finale of the land swindle.

"Pack saddles in good shape?"

"Yes, they are," said Patrick.

"What about the lash ropes?" His grandfather stared at the neat stacks of gear.

"Yup."

"Manties?"

"Plenty and in good repair."

"We still have those canvas britchens?"

"I had them changed over to leather. They were galling the horses. And I changed to wider cinches on the deckers so we can get away from circulation sores."

"The game is going to move in this snow. We ought to start thinking about heading out. If I get a good elk, I can rent a locker at Deadrock Meat and walk down every day for my game. I'll have all of the good and none of the bad. How you plan to shoe that string?"

"Two of them are plates, like Leafy. I'm just going to reset them. One's that gelding I pack salt on. Who you going to ride?"

"Harry Truman. I want heel and toe calks on him."

"I'll shoe him today, then, so you can get him rode a little before we take him in the hills. He's been turned out all summer."

The grandfather went up top with a halter and bucket of grain to catch Harry Truman. Like his namesake, Harry Truman was half thoroughbred and half mustang. He was a good horse and the last horse the old man broke.

While Patrick looked for his apron and shoeing tools, he tried to think about Claire. He had to assume she was not in trouble; but returning to a home after having called your husband's bluff with three prostitutes was not to arrive upon an exact bed of roses. Then, too, it was she who had to drive them home, laminating her own guilt with their doubtless enthusiastic tales of comparison as to their evening with Tio, a man who waited in an empty house for her return. With this thought Patrick *was* worried, and he was heartsick.

"Hello?"

"It's Patrick. Can you talk?"

"No."

"Okay, good-bye, but call me."

"Thank you so much! We have all the subscriptions we can handle!"

She hung up.

Well, she's alive and in good voice, I would say. The snow kept falling. The bunkhouse looked increasingly like some bit of Holland ceramic, its hard angles sentimental in the white down-floating crystal. Who could be against that? Patrick was slightly against it because he had to shoe Harry Truman. But Harry was a good horse, a big strong roan with just a touch of mustang jugheadedness, but strong in all quarters and surefooted to the last degree. Shoeing him, feeling the smart horse balance on three legs, as opposed to him hanging all over you like a less bright horse, Patrick felt that he could entrust him with his grandfather to the farthest, stormiest ridge.

Peculiarly, his love of the disagreeable old man emerged in the task. He used a hoof gauge to shorten the angle of the horse's front feet, so that they would break over easier, make the horse handier. He rasped everything off to the gauge and pared out the inside of the hoof, tapering his strokes to the contours of the frog, sensing with his knife the extraordinary blood-pumping dome beneath. He shod with Diamond oughts all the way around, calks at heel and toe. And when he walked him on his lead shank, the horse traveled out balanced and square. Patrick's back was sore, but he knew his grandfather could fork old Truman without concern now and spend his whole mind on the Absaroka he loved.

In Patrick's life, at times of crisis, he had sometimes wished to throw up and go to sleep. He had often wondered about this; but as he was one who despised psychiatry, no easy explanations were available to him. He thought he felt a little queasy as he dialed Claire.

"How are you?"

"Fine. Now can you talk?"

"Yes."

"I want to throw up and go to sleep."

"*What?*"

"It's snowing."

"But what did you just say?"

"I"—clears throat—"you."

"You what me?"

"Nothing."

"Hey, buddy, you're a phone crank."

"Just wanted to call."

"The telephone is an instrument which can be abused."

"Well, here's me."

"Come on, Patrick." Then she just said, "Patrick."

"I don't know. Took Grandpa to town. I'm just feeling, uh, weird."

"Why?"

"*Why!* The answer is . . ."

"The answer is what, Patrick?"

"Stress-related. I fear purgatory at the very least."

"But what *is* it?"

"I'm looking for a reason."

"I'm looking for a reason too."

"How did Tio take to the wall of hookers?"

"Not at all."

"*What?* Incidentally, where is he?"

"Right outside this window. He's trying to read my lips. He's shoveling the walk. No. Where was I? Oh, right, he wouldn't have anything to do with them. He stayed upstairs and watched Johnny Carson. *They* made quiche Lorraine and *I* had to clean up the mess."

"Well, I really never saw why we were bringing your husband three hookers."

"And it bothers you . . ."

"I think so."

"It bothers you in a way you can't quite put your finger on?"

"That's it," he said.

"I can answer that for you. Despite that it was a gesture which I thought would best help him to see how I thought he was treating me, the main thing you're worried about was whether or not it indicated some lingering passion between Tio and me."

"The crowd jumped to its feet as his teeth soared into deep left."

"What?"

"It's fair."

"What've you been smoking, son?"

"I ain't smokin. I can barely get out of my own tracks. My foot is stuck in the spittoon. I can no longer sneak up. They can hear the spittoon ringing from a mile out. By the time I get there, all that's left is tracks. And you can't smoke tracks."

Thus another one seemed drain-bound.

In the beginning was sadness; immediately after that was sadness-for-no-reason; and beyond that was the turf of those for whom the day-to-day propositions for going on at all seemed not at all to the point. Patrick, the tank man, took the middle ground: He didn't know why he felt as he did.

Why do I feel as I do?

She hung up on him. A dangerous lip-reader was shoveling her walk.

37

Heart Bar
Monday

Dear Mother,

Well, things are still in kind of a wreck around here. I have not been feeling entirely right about my behavior and I think that Dale was correct in saying that that rests upon my shoulders. Still, with us, all was not as it should have been. And I can't help but think that Mary paid the biggest part of the price. I'm not saying anybody killed her. But couldn't we have done a better job? I mean, it was quite hard to find anybody to talk to around here. It still is. Grandpa is about as chatty and agreeable as ever.

I don't know what Mary had. I had Marion Easterly but she was invisible. Afterwards I had soccer and my tank. But these things don't add up always. I met Mary's close friend of the Cheyenne persuasion and I couldn't help but thinking he had done rather more for her than her family.

He met her in a whorehouse where she had a job.

Also, I don't think Dad's airplane stunts, including the whopper in the end, were that funny.

I've been thinking about throwing in with more oil-type people, one in particular, as this high lonesome plays out right after its use in calendar photos, funnies and radio serials. I've met a nice girl.

I've found a lovely flat for the Granddad. There's a sign-language study center next door and a monorail to the emergency room. His movie hopes run higher than ever. I've persuaded him of the need of a regular physical, as well as a long hard look at the daily stool. I think he's listening up pretty fair.

Well, this is no more than an apologetic valentine to you and Dale. Tell Andrew that I feel very strongly that he will never find an arrowhead.

Think of us!

Love,
Captain Fitzpatrick

❖ 38 ❖

"TIO?" PATRICK HELD THE PHONE SLIGHTLY AWAY FROM HIS head.

"How's Patrick?"

"I'm fine."

"What can I do you for?"

"You know when we talked earlier?"

"Yes," said Tio. "Sure do. But we finished that conversation."

"Well, not entirely."

"Yeah, we did. Now, don't y'all be stupid. I've got to ease up on this beast with my rocks and sling. So don't go to jumping me out with some Yankee love of truth. Guy in my position needs to exact some teeny form of retribution without resorting to a bunch of bald statements and unusual self-righteous Yankee speeches, calling me up in the middle of the day with y'mouth hanging open, this man-to-

man horseshit, which you have my invitation to give back
to the Army."

"I can't understand this."

"Myself!"

"How does it turn out?"

"You just shake and it's snake eyes time after time.
They're loaded."

"Meaning what?"

"You never answered me about Claire."

Patrick was not used to this form of evangelical yam-
mering, if indeed anyone was. The best gloss of Tio's
speech he could come up with went: There are things one
doesn't say; in which case, they had just had a rather
traditional moment together, man-to-man, in vacant
splendor.

❖ **39** ❖

IN TIMES OF GREAT TRIBULATION, A VISIT TO MARION
Easterly often seemed important. Mary claimed that
Marion had been his greatest love, that no one would ever
equal her in Patrick's eyes. But Patrick was sure that they
had been apart long enough now, that the Miss Palm side
of Marion had sufficiently diminished and that his new
and real love for Claire was deep enough that a chat with
Marion wouldn't do all that much harm.

Marion was living with a Lutheran clergyman on Custer Street. They had a white marriage and a view of the
mountains. An irrigation overflow babbled through the
childless lawn. Or, rather, a trout-filled brook. Anyway,
babbled.

"Heck," said Patrick. "You're only a hop, skip and a jump away from Loretta's place."

"I know, but I'd be afraid those little dickenses would . . . ensnare me!"

"You could be right." Patrick had made a big Dagwood sandwich. He was trying to eat this three-decker in the fetal position without getting mayonnaise on the bed.

He told Marion that he was in love. He told her that his lady was married to a man of the oil. He mentioned that they had gone all the way and that he thought that the man of oil knew this. Marion raised her hands to the sides of her face, pretty as a picture. "Oh, oh," she exclaimed. "I fear very much for you at the hands of this person of oil."

In the afternoon Patrick expelled two West Coast coyote hunters from the ranch. They had started out on the Mojave, hoping to set a record that would make one of the gun magazines. They were, respectively, a Sheetrocker and a Perfataper. They had been taking amphetamines for four days and had nearly filled their powerful Land Cruiser with dead coyotes. The Sheetrocker did most of the driving, while the Perfataper stood through a "shooting station," which was kind of a sun roof. He had a two-sixty-four magnum and his best lick was blasting. They were four pelts shy of the record and were just working their way east, broadcasting the squeals of dying rabbits from speakers mounted behind the grill. They hadn't had a good day since the Wasatch range in Utah. They were losing weight, running out of money and pills. The Sheetrocker said that he just wanted to touch one off. And the Perfataper said not just one; we're taking a hard run at the statistics.

"Well, your dead-rabbit record is scaring my horses."

"So?"

"And you're on my land."

"So?"

Patrick thought about mayhem; but again, that could cheat him of Claire. He directed the coyote hunters up to Tio's ranch. The yellow Land Cruiser rolled off and in a moment began spitefully broadcasting the deathsqueals of the rabbits again.

Patrick wondered why he had sent them to Tio's ranch. It was not to create further trouble, certainly. Searching his mind, he decided that it became impossible to call over there again; and just maybe he could elicit some response with these yo-yos in the Jap land-gobbler.

Very generously, Catches had had the film developed of the cat stalking moths in Grassrange. In most of them the cat was a light-struck incubus figure, the light something like a separate galaxy, and the moths strangely technological creatures, as aerodynamic and systems-ridden as ICBMs. Patrick thought this was a lovely gift and hoped that the wherewithal had come from the night of Loretta, Deirdre and Tana. The letter said, "What are you doing?"

Patrick decided that in the Castilian walk-up he could go native. He would wear his hair swept back from the forehead and hold his black tobacco cigarette out at the ends of his fingertips. He would bring the pimentos back in the oiled paper, the anchovies and the terribly young lamb. He'd go to the odd mass or two, not in *preparation*, as he might now in the remorseless West; but in the healthy, ghoulish attendance of Spain, to stare at the wooden blood and pus of the old Stations of the Cross. He could have fun there and not have foreboding. He could have the time of his life making smart salads by the stone sink. It could be tops in mindless. He could duck the English secretaries like the plague, as each had already been hopelessly wounded by her own London travel agent. In any case, his crude post-coital bathrobe slopping about was sure to cause *no harm* to anyone; and the question of smelly imbroglios starring oil-minded Southwesterners could not happen to him, stainless in Madrid, with day help. The black olives in the salad would have wrinkles like the faces of men who have lived a long time, innocent of violence.

"What have you done!"

"Oh dear."

"I have narrowly escaped with my life!"

"I see it now. I said the wrong thing." Patrick was thinking of his conversation with Tio.

"You sure did."

"Give me the headlines."

"Well, they rolled in and shot everything that moved. They're in the living room now, knocking back Turkey and getting too close to Tio for comfort."

"Wait a minute. What are you talking about?"

"The coyote hunters."

"Have you talked to Tio?"

"Not yet. But he's crazy *about* them. He's in there yelling First Amendment and States' Rights. They're real drunk and it's getting crude."

"You haven't talked to him . . ."

"I talked to him right up till the coyote hunters and that was all she wrote. He said he might make a trip today in the helicopter. But if he didn't, I'd of wished he had."

"Did you know that Tio and I spoke?"

"No, I didn't."

"I'm not sure what was said. But I think we agreed you and I were sleeping together and we wouldn't talk about it."

"Do you really think that?" Claire asked in an exhalation of terror.

"I'm afraid I do."

"I better start running, then. I better clear out."

She rang off in panic. Had Patrick endangered her? He thought to himself, I'd better not have. That would have been well beyond the jaggedness-of-the-everyday.

Something was making him feel that he had touched something he didn't completely understand. He had once, washing dishes, reached deep into the suds and been flattened by electrical shock. The root system of the China willow had carried a power line into the septic tank. From Patrick's point of view, the tree had nearly electrocuted him. It took a plumber and an electrician to explain the occasion. Patrick said, "I was only washing dishes."

The plumber said, "When lightning flew out your ass."

Something about Tio was like washing those dishes.

❖ 40 ❖

CLAIRE ARRIVED AND SAID THAT THE RANCH WOULDN'T DO. The same applied to hotels, motels, rest stops and locally notorious zones of cohabitation.

"How about a johnboat?"

"No."

"Wait a minute, wait a minute. Did I do the wrong thing? Can't you say you want to be with me?"

"I just don't want to get nailed in the crosswalk."

They ended up at the line shack on Silver Stake. Patrick rammed and jammed his way in there, missing the vacant shafts, in his truck. Meadowlarks showered out of the buckbrush at the advent of grill and bumper. The combination to the lock, hanging on the warped plank pine door, was that of Marion Easterly: four zeros; easy to remember. The roof was made from sheets of aluminum used in the newsprint process. A practiced eye could invert them to the unweathered, unoxidized side and find the same old crap in aluminum immemorial. Dog eats baby. Indiana woman gives birth to five-pound bass. Silver Stake was on the Heart Bar allotment. The walls were made of the miserable little east-slope logs with their millions of pin knots. It had a patent heater and a pack rat bunk. It was kind of a cowboy joint, hidden upside a terrific wilderness. Patrick missed his Charlie Parker records.

He missed Bud Powell as well, despite recent associations. He did have the following to protect Guinevere from storm and flood: one sledge, two splitting wedges, a double-bitted axe, kitchen matches, Winchester, twenty rounds Remington Core-Lokt 140 grain, Pabst Blue Ribbon (a case), potatoes, onions, stew beef, fifty-pound sack of pinto beans ("I've got to stock up for fall roundup! I am *not* making an an an assumption!"), peppers and pepper derivatives—Frank's Louisiana hot sauce, ancho peppers, chilipiquines and Tabasco. Blankets: five-line Hudson Bay, two. Artilleryman's gloves. Harry Truman biography: "When I hear them praying in the amen corner, I head home to lock the smokehouse." Something like that.

"Why do we have all this stuff?"

"It's our new life!"

"What!"

Drip-baste cast-iron pot; skillet *con* giant flapjack flipper; and the requisite lid from an old Maytag washing machine. Soap: laundry, dish and personal. Steel wool. Dry rack, dish set with bluebirds, and percolator.

"It looks like we're here to stay! And we're not!"

Patrick gave the lock the full zeros and they were inside. Rat manure and newspaper bits were strewed on the adzed floor timbers. From the window one little turn of Silver Stake Creek turned up to the right and disappeared like a live comma. It was a world that yielded only to a broom, flung-open windows and wood smoke. They threw the flypaper out in the snow with its horrid quarter-pound load of dead flies. Thermal inversion pushed the first smoke down the chimney, and then the flue heated and sucked. There were empty cartridges on the windowsill, a calendar that didn't work this year and a coyote skull for a soap holder. Next to the sink was a cheap enamel pitcher, in flecked white and gray, for dishwater.

"God, I don't know," said Claire. "Are we preparing a moonlit rendezvous?"

"I really don't know, either. You said you wanted to get out of town."

"But this has the earmarks of a shack-up. What I had in mind was my life. Saving of same. I wanted to miss the initial flash. Hold me. There. Oh dear, Patrick. What in God's name did you do?"

Patrick split up the small fatty pine chunks for the woodstove. "I've been trying to think why I did that. Honestly, I thought it was what you would have insisted upon. Not a shack-up. I know it's a shack, but . . . well."

"Again."

"What?"

"Hold me." He could feel her wary, wild shape through her clothes.

They stood in the cool cabin, the pine beginning to catch and the fog of condensation starting to spread on the cold windows; the awful, clear mountain light diminished and modulated its measuring-stick quality, its cartoon illumination of human events. The cabin filled with golden light, finally; the stove crackled and the cold fall sun hung, suspended and inglorious, in the steamy glass. The minute bough tips of evergreen touched the same glass, casting spidery black shadows in the steam.

Sling the mattress over on the coil springs, to the side upon which no pack rat has trod. Claire made up the bunk with the woolen blanket so that it looked like a Pullman berth on a silver shadow train flying through the Carolinas in last light. Claire was a bow beneath him, thumbs indenting his arms, intense this side of screaming. Then her face tipped to one side. And Patrick stared down at her strong bare body as he entered again and again. He wanted to say that sufficiency rather than salvation was at issue. Then, jetting into her, there swept over him an indifference to their danger. Therefore, he shut the hell up and for the moment was glad to be home.

Blanket over his shoulders, Patrick attended to the interior of the little ship set against the hard evergreens, now throwing the peculiar pulsing light of a pressure lantern through the imperfect windows. He took the claw hammer and, clutching the blanket around himself as though modesty continued to be an issue, battered down the exposed nails that years of frost had heaved up out of the flooring. He put perhaps more effort into this than it entirely required.

"Patrick, Tio was my neighbor in Oklahoma. His mother virtually raised me. We'd hit it pretty good and there wasn't time for us kids at our house. There wasn't a thing wrong with him, there really wasn't. Anyway, I married him. And then after that—and maybe this is where I feel like I broke with something I never should have—after that, I took up with my people's views. Which is not necessarily bad in and of itself; but the situation was that I had all the leverage and pretty soon we weren't in high school and we weren't at A & M and then we weren't even in Tulsa. And pretty soon it was pretty damned fast and I had broken his heart one too many times. But by the time I was sorry there was something there in him that was gone for good."

"How had you broken his heart one too many times?"

"That will never be any of your business."

Patrick thought, You are in your perfect little cabin, which you have seen as a ship on an empty sea; and the light and the air seem to substantiate your happiness as you putter around in your wigwam blanket tapping back nails. And then there is something not unlike the blind flash experienced by those whose homes have suddenly been illuminated by the voluminous and unwelcome light of a flamethrower, or some self-immolating madman who picked your yard, or a bad wire, a meteor, an act of God . . . gasoline.

Patrick said, "That's enough for me. I don't want to hear any more."

"To start with, Tio was all right. But he's not all right anymore."

"What was all right about him? I don't want to hear this."

"He had just so much talent but he busted a gut for that. And about the two thousandth storage tank my people tried to shove down his throat, his mind quit that little bit, and in Tio's mind he was an oilman. Then he had airplanes, stewardesses and guns. He learned to farm things out. He bought everything he wore at Cutter Bill's

in Dallas. He never rode a horse but now he couldn't miss
Ruidoso. He began to speak of his daddy. His daddy was
what you'd call an Okie with a capital O, little ole thin-
lipped Ford parts manager out at the four corners. Despite his redneck ways, he always wanted Tio to buckle
when it came to those tanks, however many fourflushers,
missed connections or falsified airline tickets that might
have entailed."

"This has grown too heavy. This is becoming quite
brutal. And anyway, all I wanted was your ass." His
throat grabbed.

"C'mere, Mr. Wretch."

"No, now wait a minute."

"For what. Give me the blanket, anyway." She began to
sing. It had become obvious that she was, to a highly
refined degree, hysterical. " 'I've been to Redwood, I've
been to Hollywood—' "

"Oh, stop this. Stop!"

But by then she was crying and Patrick could only
stand by, stove heat to his back, wrapped in his dopy
blanket.

"Please stop."

So a night passed without much sleep; then just before
light a lynx screamed in the rocks and Patrick got up to
fire the stove once again, preparing to make breakfast. He
stopped to reach under the blanket, which was pulled
over Claire's head, and with the morning hands of a
sleepy cook, examined her entire body, just to do that,
before she could wake up. He held his hands against his
face, then cracked the eggs one by one, watching them
drop into the white bowl. He stared at them. The vague
anticipatory birds, too small to shoot, the ones that ruin
all-nighters, began to make specific announcements from
the surrounding brush. When he went out to the creek to

fill the percolator, the stony air stung Patrick's skin. And as soon as the first brown bubble appeared in the glass top, he slipped back under the blanket to rediscover Claire's expectant and dreaming heat.

Patrick put breakfast on the table. The cabin was warm now. He could think of only one fact: Nobody knows where we are. But we've been here overnight and that is a declaration.

"This is extremely wonderful, Patrick."

"Thank you."

"I'm worried."

"I know you must be. But if we could suspend that—"

"Let's try. We shall see us try."

They made a decent attempt at making an island of the place, like an English couple eating marmalade in an air raid. Patrick had parked the truck nearly against the cabin in case the lantern inside didn't work; but when he glanced up and saw the one headlight in the window, it frightened him for an instant. He thought, With all my reputation for independence and for being warlike, it would seem I'm afraid of everything; it was one of the secrets he had that he had never cared to keep. But now he wanted to be courageous, because without it he had no chance of holding Claire. There were so many questions about her existence that would have to have help; and it was Patrick who had brought everything to a head with his codified silences with Tio. Hiding in the woods wasn't going to do for long. Lastly, he realized it was the headlight of his own truck.

"Let me ask you something," he said, testing his bravery. "Do you love me?"

"Yes."

"Very well. I know what I'm going to do. I'm going to go see Tio."

At this point there were no gestures that could accompany such extreme statements. It just had to be said across the table. Anyway, Patrick was going. He didn't look sure of himself and Claire seemed too depleted to respond.

❖ **41** ❖

PATRICK'S HEART WAS POUNDING WHEN HE CLIMBED FROM the truck. He deliberately walked past the front window so that he could glance inside. The Cadillac was tilted up on the slope to the lawn; and he remembered that that was where he had seen it last—a precise parking habit. But mainly he noticed the huge tire prints of some powerful machine across the new lawn in a big arc that took them out of the place—not down the road but directly out through the sagebrush. Then, he noticed the flies on the window, thousands of them.

He knocked without getting an answer. So he knocked again. He craned to see past the angle of the hallway into the kitchen, but could discern nothing. He tried the door and found it open. He walked in among coatracks festooned with deluxe sporting clothes and was overpowered by some awful smell. He was completely frightened, but he worked his way into the kitchen, calling out Tio's name ahead of himself through the kitchen and into the living room.

The living room was ruined with broken bottles and glasses, turned-over furniture and, worst of all, the carcasses of coyotes, some skinned so that they looked alive, veined and bug-eyed, in reaching-out postures so distinctive as to suggest they ran even in death. Hides, curled up and stinking, one hanging on the ninth largest whitetail ever killed in Texas, all swam under a mantle of flies. Patrick rolled open the windows and turned the heat off.

He started upstairs; and by the landing he could see Tio's boots, toes down over the top step. Patrick thought, He's dead. He climbed the rest of the way, and as he moved around Tio's rumpled body, the body moved, the head turned up for a look. "Fitzpatrick."

"What's the problem here, Tio?"

"Had some bounty-hunter friends on a visit. Godamighty, did I sleep here?"

"Evidently you did."

Tio struggled into a kneeling position and let his head hang for a long moment. "Godamighty. Last thing I remember, we was trying to get them coyotes skinned. We was a little far gone." Tio got up. "I was shooting at something in the fireplace. I guess they panicked. Up till then, our plan was to hunt you down like an animal. Which is all you are. Then I had kind of a fit and they run off on me."

Tio wandered toward the bathroom and closed the door. Patrick expected him to emerge with a gun. He looked around the room for the weapon Tio had mentioned and didn't see it. He began to be sure that it was in the bathroom. Then he heard the shower running. In the eerie situation it sounded like some kind of weather behind the closed bathroom door, like a distant storm that ended suddenly. Patrick then thought of Claire, on the chance his minutes were numbered.

The bathroom door swung open. Tio, wrapped in a towel, was drawing broad stripes through the shaving cream on his face. Still standing at the top of the stairs, Patrick could hear the sleepy drone of the flies downstairs. Tio spoke to him, shaving accurately and without a mirror.

"Eat up with the dumb ass," he said, grimly.

"Looks like it."

"*What* . . . in the fuck are you doing here?"

This sent Patrick spinning: Was it to lay claim to the first thing he seemed prepared to fight for since coming home? Was it to bring to closure a mystery he couldn't bear in all the tranquility of the cabin? He really didn't know; but he understood that those were the questions.

"Well, Claire got kind of frightened by your guests."

"That's not it," said Tio, leaning over the sink and scrubbing vigorously at his teeth. I've got it, thought Patrick, I'll tell Claire I shot him. No, Christ, that's hysterical. Tio stood and turned toward him. "You could drive to my house, but you couldn't tell me the truth. Pitiful. I'm supposed to need professional supervision, but you're pitiful." He threw the towel behind and wandered naked to the closet, where he took the utmost care in picking his wardrobe for the day: Levis, a green chambray shirt and his tall boots. The buckle on his belt had the cat-track brand overlaid on it in gold. It was Claire's family brand. Patrick was relieved he'd gotten his clothes on. And he was still thinking about being called pitiful. He felt his blood rise.

"I love Claire," he said.

"Oh, I bet you do."

"That doesn't seem important to you?"

"I'd hate to see you get her killed. *That's* important to me. I'm crazy about the girl."

"What are you talking about?"

"Well, you say you're in love with her. How would you like some clown putting her life in question?"

"I wouldn't."

"Well, as the lady's husband, I'm here to tell you that that is exactly what you're doing. Nothing will happen to you. You're not important enough and nobody is going to *make* you important enough. Otherwise this little turn with Claire would look like it meant something, and it don't. It's just a momentary case of the dumb ass. Basically, we're up north on vacation and maybe it got a little rowdy. Oklahoma can be brutal hot in the summertime. But it's starting to cool off now. It's time Claire and me headed home. So you fetch her. Tio's gonna carry her back to where being with her people makes her feel bulletproof again."

Patrick started down the stairs ahead of Tio, and just as they moved to the level of the flies, he heard a sudden noise behind him, one that revealed the fear within himself, and the gasped word *"Fitzpatrick."* Patrick turned and saw Tio half-seated, half-sprawled on the steps above him. He was changing color quickly and had lost control of his body. A stain spread at his crotch and Patrick could see in his struggling eyes that he now could no longer speak. Patrick remembered Claire's words: *"I'm the doctor and Tio is the patient and you are a cruel outsider."* Was this it?

Tio was lighter than Patrick had expected. He carried him to the truck in the crazy daylight and felt the gusts of Tio's malady. Then, on the drive to the hospital, Tio twisted up against his door and his teeth began rattling against the window. Patrick pulled him upright and kept on driving.

They wheeled Tio through emergency. The doctor on call said they'd had him once before, explaining this while he tapped the nail of his forefinger on the crystal of his wristwatch. He held the watch to his ear and directed

Patrick to the lobby to check Tio in. Tio glided off, wheeled by an orderly, his tall boots immobilized by a retaining strap. His face was locked in some terrible rictus, but his eyes blazed toward Patrick; Patrick would never forget their blaze.

Patrick checked him in, writing Claire's name under "Next of Kin" and his own on the bottom line.

❖ 42 ❖

ON THE WAY BACK TO SILVER STAKE CREEK, PATRICK STOPPED at his ranch and put the stock rack on his truck. He loaded Leafy and Box L, saddles, picket ropes and a hundred pounds of sweet feed. He went inside to see how his grandfather was doing and found the place in good order. He discovered the old man in the living room watching Houston play Denver.

"Hey, Grandpa, I'm running—"

"Where?"

"I'm spending time with a real great lady."

"I'm glad to hear that."

"But look, I want to make early elk with you. So will you do me a favor? Will you buy us our groceries? I'll be back to get us packed in four or five days."

"What do you want to eat?"

"You decide. And get me a box of 270's. Hundred thirty grain."

"How long you plan to stay with this young lady?"

"I told you, four or five days. Nothing is forever."

Then he headed south. He could see Leafy's mane streaming in the rear-view mirror, Box L turning his forehead into it. Sixty-mile-an-hour horses with a highway unraveling behind them.

The mountains paralleled the valley and the snowy peaks were extending with fall to the valley floor. Patrick wondered seriously if this country had ever been meant to be lived in. Right now he could only imagine small hot spots of survival, winter seemed so imminent. He could imagine lying in bed with Claire and he could imagine seeing after his grandfather on the ranch and diligently looking after his warm animals so that the cold didn't sweep them away. But the country lacked the detailed human regimen he imagined he could find in his Castilian walk-up, daily human rituals of coffee, cigarettes, wine, newspapers. The Deadrock region was just exactly the dumb fucking dehumanized photogenic district that would require a bunch of American reformed Protestants to invent. His mood had begun to show.

Patrick was getting sour; he was getting ready to cheat. He drove up into the brush once more. There was still some smoke at the head of the chimney; so he'd done that right. He unloaded Leafy, then Box L. He drove picket pins out in the meadow and hobbled them so they wouldn't cross lines.

And then he went inside. Claire had taken down the Hudson Bay and was curled, undressed, in front of the wood stove.

"Tell me," she said.

"He's gone."

"Gone? Gone where?"

"It said Tulsa."

"*What* said Tulsa?"

"The note. It said he would be back by hunting season. I'm taking my grandfather in the hills then. And you can go. Or whatever you decide." All Patrick could think in the indescribable panic that touched him was, I'm sure he's getting the best of care. He's going to have to live a few days without her at the side of his bed.

Claire smiled. "Then we have some time together," she said.

"I wish we had a lot of time together."

"We don't, darling. Let's not pine for what we don't have."

Patrick thought, I've lied my way into this. What ever happened to the officer and the gentleman? He concluded that it had never been the case. The hell with it. "What are we to make of this?"

"I think we're going to have a perfect time," said Claire. "I'm real encumbered, but I'm falling in love with you."

"That's what's happening to me."

"Isn't it so nice?"

"I don't know if those are the words," he said.

Shortly thereafter, packing saddlebags to take some limited supplies to the divide, the horses tied nose to nose at wind-twisted spruce next to the creek, Patrick knew that he was going to have to say something. But he was determined not to say it now. Otherwise the police or the papers or some blind, abstract party would do the work for him. So he was going to have to say something.

When they got to the top of the world where the lichen made free, unearthly effects, as though the rocks were stained by sky, they tied the horses once more, loosened cinches and made love on cold ground where spring flowers were blooming in the mouth of winter. Then they tied a knot at the corners of the Hudson Bay and enclosed themselves in it, though the blanket now smelled of the four-thousand-foot pull just made by Leafy and Box L.

"The thing is this: When I got to the house, the thing is, Tio was there, actually."

"He was? You say he was there?"

"And at first things seemed quite normal. He just insisted that I be removed from this situation and that way this would never have happened. I didn't think I saw him overwrought. He showered and changed. And suddenly he'd fallen and it was kind of . . . a fit."

"Why didn't you tell me?"

"I wanted the time with you."

"What's the matter with him? You liar!"

"I don't know." He was stung.

"Did they get him to the hospital?"

"I took him."

"You were there when he fell apart? He's not going to like that."

"Does he always come out of these?"

"Yes. I wish you hadn't lied to me."

"Well, I just did," said Patrick angrily.

"Is he hurt?"

"No, and the doctor on emergency had seen him before. So I thought they'd know what to do."

"They will. But it doesn't show up on the brain scan or in blood tests. And it never happened before we married."

"That could just be coincidence."

"It's not. But you didn't tell me the truth."

"Are you entirely guilty for these fits? Is that your opinion?"

Patrick's question sent Claire on a jag, as though somehow it all had to be pinned down immediately or their own fortunes would be swept under by the same malady.

"My family persuaded Tio that I had married beneath myself. I could have prevented Tio from believing that. I assure you he was a very nice boy and he bought what my

family had to say. Tio never looked up from the work my
father had set him to do until he had proven he was a
genuine Tulsa *patrón* just like my father. It took years.
And when Tio returned his attentions to me, I just wasn't
really there anymore. He began saying peculiar things.
And when my father was dying, Tio hung around his hospital room. He said he wanted to be in at the death. He
succeeded, the only one to see the so-called final gasp.
Then, sir, we went on a tear: Ruidoso, Santa Fe, Vail, La
Paz. I didn't know whether he was happy or sad. He
didn't know if I was there with him or not, and it just
lingered like that until we started on home from Palm
Springs. Tio stood up in front of the in-flight movie and
went haywire. He was horrible and superhuman and we
had to make an emergency landing in Phoenix. They had
this center where they could study him, and let's see, I
think it was there that he asked me whether or not I was
going to let him go under. And I said I wouldn't. Two
days later, he was pounding that WATS line. And like
I said, it's not on the brain scan or in the blood tests. But I
did say I wouldn't let him go under. I hope you've got
that clear."

They didn't come down from the divide until darkness
had fallen and the shining mantle of stars had rotated into
the night. The stars looked like matches. There was some
word for matches that was very close to the word "lucifer."
They looked like lucifers; and the horses picked down
over the blasted rocks. You couldn't see their legs and
down in the trees Patrick and Claire couldn't see each
other and the lucifers were hidden behind the branches
and even in the cold you waited for the lightning. "It
would be hard for us to be much of anything with that

hanging over us," Claire said, almost asking. Patrick felt the sickness overcome him, the sickness he had known, one way or another, would come. "Tio knows me very well. He studied very closely and saw me falling in love with you. And I'm the one who made him so mean." Leafy slid on the granite veil that caught the vague light of stars; and sparks streamed from her iron shoes. "What do you wish?" Claire asked.

"I wish you'd shut up."

LOITERING BEFORE THE HOSPITAL SEEMED NOT THE IDEAL thing. Pacing like an expectant father, he had less than the routine beatitude upon his face. Presently Claire emerged, and from an unofficial doorway, suggesting familiarity with the place.

"He's resting. He's completely conscious."

"What did he say?"

"He said that he was surprised to see me and that he thought I had come because I found sick people amusing."

"He's lost none of his sense of humor. Did he tug at your heartstrings?"

"Somewhat." Her eyes clouded over as she turned to gaze at Patrick. A doctor arrived on a ten-speed bicycle and shot past very close, so that for a moment the air was filled with bay rum.

"Let's go."

They drove toward Claire's place. Patrick told her about the condition of its interior, the carcasses, the bottles.

Claire turned on the radio. *"The girls all look prettier at closing time."* "I wish things would lighten up," she said. "I know we're grown and all. But I'd like to dance my ass off."

"Tell me about it."

"We'll survive this. But what is that worth?"

Patrick remembered Germany when the drugged girls were carried screaming from the cafés, the sense of flames in the doorways, the nerve net hanging vulnerable in empty space. Now the space was turning to enclosure and that was probably what Claire meant by wanting to dance her ass off. He wasn't sure; but it had her quality of saying the right thing.

She was not prepared for the inside of the house. While Patrick raced around filling plastic bags, Claire flung open the windows, upstairs and down. Soon the wind coursed through the place, carrying flies and stink to blue eternity. When Patrick went upstairs he could see a shadow below, just as when Tio had paced the night of their dinner. At the top of the stairs was a photograph of Claire's wedding. She looked quite the same, except that in the photograph she wore her hair in an old-fashioned chignon; but perhaps that was just the style of wedding pictures, the photographer hoping to give his work a lasting quality by suggesting the newlyweds had died some time ago.

The curtains in the big bedroom stood straight out the window in the breeze. Reports fluttered under paperweights. Claire made the bed with fresh sheets and said, "Would you like to stay with me tonight?"

There was no sense that her husband haunted the room, and Patrick said yes. Then they stopped the chores and sat in the window seat holding hands. They could see down to the meadows. The hay had recently been mown and lay in windrows drying and waiting to be baled. They looked at the varied yellow triangles as closely as if they awaited something crossing them. What could that have been? No telling; but it did seem the setting for a mythical creature or a fugitive.

"May I see your breasts?"

Claire smiled and undid her shirt, dropping it around her waist without untucking it from her pants. Patrick's heart pounded. They were small and definite, like a girl's; and their pallor against the tan of her shoulders and face made them seem secret and powerful. She pulled her shirt on. "Chilly."

"Thank you."

"Hadn't you looked before?"

"I was swept away."

"I see. So was I."

"Does one ever just say the hell with it?"

"The hell with what?" she asked.

"The consequences."

"Some people do," she said, without much warmth for those people.

"Did you ever want someone so much you didn't make love because you'd be too close to see them?"

"That hasn't happened, but I think it's not impossible. I guess that would be adoration."

A harrier hawk flew low against the meadows, banking and casting on new angles in the wind.

"How much of you is there left?" Patrick asked.

"I'd be the last to know. How much of you is left?"

"Well, my major foray into self-pity is the belief that it's all left," Patrick said.

"I certainly don't have *that* belief. You have to have lost a thing or two along the way."

"Please don't say that."

"Okay, but you're a very silly boy. And certainly don't embarrass yourself for me by listing the things you've lost and left behind."

"It's fair."

"So it's agreed, we're going dancing."

"I'd love to," said Patrick, lying reversed on the bed, leaning on his elbows, facing Claire's closet. Claire was trying on clothes for him. She had immense vanity, enhanced by the sunny pleasure she took from it. Patrick thought, *I could never make this up.* He tried to puzzle out the pretty petulance of women picking through their clothes, as though every blouse, every slip or dress, seemed to personally let them down a little. Claire held a spangled silk blouse up to her eyes and said, "What in the world could I have been thinking?" Finally she lay on the floor to pull on a pair of tight jeans. She put on a pair of rose-and-silver high-heeled shoes, a silver belt and a loose silk top with short sleeves. This had all been quite measured. Patrick was cotton-mouthed.

"And you mustn't get terribly drunk."

"I won't."

"And if I see you starting, I will ask you to stop."

"How?"

"As proof of your love. As proof of how mortally serious it is to go dancing."

"Then it will work. Where shall we go?"

"The Northbranch."

That was the spot all right; but it would make an unmistakable announcement that would fly through Deadrock.

"It's not exactly a hideout."

"I'm not ashamed."

Unless you're on the dance floor under the wagon wheels and lights, you have to walk sideways in the Northbranch on a Saturday night; and inevitably, to get a drink you have to wedge into the service bar and irritate the barmaids. Then when you dance you have to leave your drink on someone's table, and it is considered to be in the tradition of the West for others to finish your drink for you while you are away.

No amount of lovemaking replaces dancing, though there's a connection. The band played "Faded Love," then "Please Release Me" and "The Window up Above." Patrick and Claire slow-danced to a fiddler with a smoky, reminiscent style and to the singing of a short man whose Stetson couldn't quite hide all his baldness and whose voice was fine and deliberate and haunting as trains in distant night.

Claire seemed strong and light as Patrick held her, curving his hand around her back and holding her hand rather formally and elevated. She rested her face straight against his chest. A few people stared; but the dancing continued, the whole crowded floor graduating slowly in a circle. Young cowboy couples with their hands in each other's back pockets and toothpicks in their hat brims; older people in fox-trot postures with crazily fixed expressions; indifferent couples counting the house or watching Patrick and Claire; a drunk in a green suit, his hand upraised, his index finger extended, trying and failing to cut in: these and others were bound to the slow circle toward the music. Patrick could feel Claire's back expand now and then with a sigh. Then some gruesome story-song commenced about dogs and children and watermelon wine. They left the floor.

They managed to find a spot at the bar. In the mirror Patrick could see Calamity Jane and remembered being here last: love and death: Claire and the sled dog Dirk. The bartender came up.

"Man wants to buy you both a drink."

"Thank you," said Patrick and ordered. "Who is it?"

"He phoned it in from the hospital. Man down there's gonna cover for him."

Man down there was Deke Patwell. Weak waves, Deke with a little painted grin. I don't know and I don't care, thought Patrick. Claire had been watching. Deke must have phoned the hospital with the latest.

"Do you want to throw up and go to sleep?" she asked.

"Not at all."

"Shall we dance?"

"Yes."

They were back in the dense wheel, a hundred faces strangely anesthetized by three cheating songs in a row. It seemed unlucky.

"How are you holding up?"

"I'm going to be able to stand it," said Claire. "Just."

"Won't you go with me somewhere a long way off?"

"No."

The little flame lights overhead lent the place a peculiar ecclesiastic air. Patrick couldn't remember why. It seemed in the Bible there were always flames dancing over things and that the flames were meant to be a positive sign. These dusty light bulbs weren't going to be quite all that. But there, after all, was Claire's imaginary precursor, the impossibly ugly Calamity Jane in the clothing of a scout. However, the latest song from the bandstand referred to two-timers as snakes crawling in the night. Patrick remembered Tio calling over the phone that he was down among the snakes; and that when you threw the dice they always came up snake eyes.

"Claire, do you fear Tio?"

"I know him too well."

"Most people are murdered by people they know well. Do you think you're in any danger from him?"

"If I am, there's nothing I can do about it."

"You sound like my sister," said Patrick; then he remembered that he had it exactly wrong, that it was Mary who had accused him of being more fatal than any Hindu. "Actually, I'm not right about that," he said. "You're more like me."

They danced from cheating to trucks to lost love to faded love again, which seemed sadder than lost love, to the green grass of home, double beds, jobs you could shove, a ride to San Antone, yellow roses, the Other One, caring and trees. Claire put her arms around him and began to cry. She said, "Oh baby, do something." When the first, most ardent wave had passed over him, he thought, and not without fear or confusion but still shot through with ardor, This is it.

"If we could only remember . . ." Patrick trailed off with the quality of dramaturgical preplanning; but then, helplessly, having at this moment seemed inauthentic even to himself, he just doggedly fell silent, because he was certain that if they both could remember any of their original intentions, *something* would occasion a rescue, something astral; but not, certainly, this assaying of present requirements. A former captain of tanks encounters a former Oklahoma golden girl still actively married to a current person of the oil, with difficulties, none of which appear on the apparatus: What values shall we assign to each, that is, from loyalty to practicality to romance? Do we subtract for the premature curtailment of tank? Do we dock for nonamplification of golden-girlism? Do we quantify our reservations as to the nondocumentable nature of oilperson's helpless flaws? How about this: Altruistic cowboy tank captain rescues princess of the Cimarron from mock-epileptic oil-and-gas-lease scoundrel. No, well . . . no. But if we could only remember. Anyway, Claire caught that, knew the long thought was genuine, even if the deck was stacked and, for her as for practically everybody, the matter of remembering first intentions was as reproachful as anything could be. The road to hell has seen more paving materials than the Appian Way, I-90 and A-1-A combined.

"Okay, let's buck up here now."

"Very well," she said.

"Are we at the crossroads?"

"I have no idea."

"Can one have fun at the crossroads?"

"I have had no reports as to that," she said.

"For instance, having disguised myself as a nurse, shall I pull Tio's various life-support connections?"

"There are none."

"But if there were."

"There aren't."

"Ball breaker."

"Now, now."

Of course, they were trying to work themselves into a reckless state of mind, a form of play in the face of grave consequences familiar to the bandits and thrill-killers of history. This time it wasn't working. It was undemonstrated that Claire lacked love for Tio. It was not clear that Patrick had a plan. Most of all, everything with respect of the heart's grave and eternal sweep seemed at odds with the constant machine-gunning of the age.

"I do love you," she said so fatally as to put it beside desolations he had already come to know, ones which played human hope against arithmetic and impossibility. Meanwhile it seemed that not only was Patrick drunk but he was about to break down. Who wanted to go dancing and put up with this?

"I know what you're thinking. But you're going to have to pull yourself together."

"What do you mean?"

"*Cheer up.*" It was the only thing she could have said to return Patrick to the ground and make him stop circulating with ghosts and faulty desire. A car crashed outside and there was a long jingle of glass, a stuck horn.

"They're playing our song," said a revitalized Patrick, sweeping Claire to the floor for a turn.

AT CLOSING TIME SHE WANTED TO BE TAKEN HOME; AND IT was clear she meant to be dropped off, that Patrick was to go to his own place. He said that he didn't understand. They were both slightly drunk. Couples swarmed past, carrying plastic to-go cups. One bartender had moved next to the door opposite the bouncer, who was sitting on a Naugahyde-and-steel kitchen chair. His thighs pressed together all the way to his knees, and he reviewed departing customers as though they were only going on parole.

Patrick started the engine. "What is this?"

"What is what?"

"Just dropping you off?"

"Time to think. I mean that, Patrick."

"You mean as if there were an answer."

"That's just what I mean."

"Well, you'll have to outgrow that," said Patrick. He meant nothing enigmatic by his remark, and in fact the notion hung over the entire ride to Claire's ranch, suggesting there *was* something to it. Therefore—though it had been a superb evening, given the time and place, most of the immediate gloom kept at bay—Claire went straight to the house. Patrick wheeled the truck's lights against the scattered buildings and suppressed an urge to go back into town and look for some kind of trouble. He was beyond that; he headed home to the Heart Bar Ranch—that is, his inheritance with its increasingly vacant buildings and rooms.

By nine in the morning he had reduced the broader effects of his hangover by ruthless scrubbing in the shower, harsh versions of the remaining ablutions, clean clothes and coffee with his grandfather.

"I forgot to send in the meter reading. So they came out and did it and charged us." His grandfather delicately tested the layer of cream on his coffee with the tip of his spoon; then he gave it a stroke and it all twirled to color. He sipped. "One guy to drive the truck. One guy to read the meter and write it down. There'll be a third person to bill us for the extra, which is five dollars. The electric company is gonna be fifty bucks in the hole."

"Everything else all right?"

"Seems so. I've been out on Truman. Everybody looks sound. One yearling pulling up a back leg. I don't see a stifle there or anything to be concerned about, though.

I've paid no attention to the irrigated ground. I shut off the wheel line and the hell with it. Seems like Truman's gaits have improved. That old dogtrot's practically a rack now. Wish I could take him to town."

An hour later, ignoring official visiting hours, he was sitting next to Tio's bed. Tio said, "This is just foolish."

"Maybe not."

"You reach a certain age, I think, when you haven't got your house in order and you start seeking out bad situations."

"You think that's what I'm doing?" Patrick asked.

"I see you as some character who joins the Foreign Legion hoping to be killed by Arabs because his dog has died. And if everything goes well and they put a bullet in him way out there on the desert, the dog is still the only one to feel sorry for."

Patrick was silenced, not simply by the creeping appropriateness of the speech, but by the glimpse of that in Tio which had drawn Claire: the character, the oil-field voodoo.

"Who do we feel sorry for in your life?" Patrick asked.

"Always been hard to say. I had begun, *once* I began, to figure out who'd had who. Got close, I mean extra close, when—snap—I started my rigor mortis routine. Never been much in the long run. Casts its little old shadow on things. Course, from a cold-ass business point of view, a guy doesn't want to weigh in as a nut. But some things can't be helped. And if I could help this, then what could I do? Kill you? Kill her? Kill myself? God works in mysterious ways, I'm a bald-ass liar if he don't. Nothing more ruinous to my expectations in life than waving a pistol around or farming out crimes that point an accusing finger at me. Slow grind don't set you in your place, then I'm a nigger aviator. Just remember this, Fitzpatrick: I've got a gadget-filled mind. And I've got a gadget for every situation."

A brilliant light—brilliant suggesting something momentary, as a flare—fell upon Patrick, who staggered very slightly and acknowledged acquaintances with a quick sideways tip of the head, a gesture he had not formerly used in America. At Front Street in the clangor of the shunting yard, he grinned to himself and thought: Rue Northern Pacific . . . Calle Caboose. Perhaps this is the caboose. The noose of the caboose. The last car before the vanishing rails, a view entirely different from that from the engine.

Everything from finding the truck to returning to Silver Stake seemed to happen at half speed. Why in a movie camera did you have to run the film through at high speed to produce slow motion? Why couldn't things happen "in a wink" as they did in the books he read as a boy? The desire to use up the road in a wink is the way the high-speed camera of the drunk's brain produces accidents, the mad wish for change.

In the last mile before camp, perhaps some admission was at hand, no sheepish acquiescence to the occasion, but an actual acknowledgment of all the signs and semaphors and general messages from headquarters that the very thing he had begun to hang his fatigued hopes upon was out of the question.

He opened his jackknife to cut the black twine on the baled prairie hay. He separated that into flakes and fed them into the small corral so that the horses could eat

well away from one another. He knocked the grain pan-
nier to scatter possible mice and brought Leafy a bucket
of oats. He sat down rather heavily before her and held
the bucket. She exhaled across his head and face question-
ingly before dropping her muzzle into the grain. She ate
with the regularity of a horse who will be fed again; and
when Patrick held his hands around the strangely delicate
pasterns, feeling the heat that arose from the coronal
bands of hoof, she stopped, pricked her ears forward,
stared with the black and endless eyes that had made him
cut her out from the other foals numerous springs ago and
went back to eating. Patrick had imagined she was worried about him, that he was somebody. Then the patterned movement, observed from this crazy angle of legs
—hoofs all as different as seashells—and the disappearance of everything into the dark: the orderly rotation of
big animals according to their decorum from feed to
water to standing sleep, a movement throughout the night
that never disturbed Patrick, sleeping face down in the
mountain corral.

Claire found him there, not before he had awakened but
before he'd had time to reconstruct and too late for him to
jump up and pretend to be doing anything else. Storewide
gala on mortification of the flesh. Patrick was sick of it but
couldn't think what there was to be done.

"I wanted to see if you were all right."

"Of course I'm all right."

"I see."

He sat up and gazed around the corral: horses, poles,
the crowding evergreen slope; how absurd, the sort of
thing to give you the sweats. Claire's hands seemed to

plunge deeper into the pockets of her blue dress. Beautiful as usual, thought Patrick angrily. In the meanwhile I've become a laugh.

"What are you doing today?" she asked tentatively. It was as if they were starting all over again.

"Reading a book."

"What book?"

"It's called *The Life of Marion Easterly* and it's by all three Brontë sisters."

He thought, I shall not be tempted by any of this. I prefer the concerned breathing of my horse upon my much-abused head in the night—though Claire would have seen to it that I went to the cabin. On the other hand, waking up and seeing there was nothing to eat, I would have gone on my own.

Creeping in was a new light-heartedness. Patrick ruefully considered that Claire might get away with this one. Just as well head indoors, then, and tidy up.

The broad-bottomed tin kettle sent clouds of steam into the room, and the stout wood stove beat gentle heat against Patrick's bare knees. There will be shaving; there will be brighter eyes. The wandering part in his hair would be rediscovered and traced to the crown of his scalp. Teeth only the madmen at Ipana could dream of. A nice shirt from the clutches of the Armed Forces in Europe. But it was pathetic.

Soon, however, they were shouting.

"*Tio seems very used to your indiscretions.*"

"*He's not.*"

"*It seems he is.*"

"Shall I just go, Patrick?"

Now he was sorry, at first because of his shouting. Then he remembered her shouting and he was less sorry. Besides, the way moods swept back and forth over lovers like tide seemed now to Patrick a humiliating process. I love you I hate you I'll kill you I can't live without you blah blah blah. This last thought took him to the final button of his shirt. He dropped his hands to his sides, watched the steam carry to the door past Claire and believed he felt like the Ancient Mariner at an abandoned bus stop. Then Claire stirred together some breakfast—a rather scientific attempt, he thought, to raise his blood sugar, going to Jerusalem with a Bible and a soil-test kit. I should start shouting the moment I've eaten my breakfast. I mean *shouting*.

"Can we ride again?"

"Let's load up and get the fuck out of here."

"This has been so lovely out here. Are we about to be actual?"

"We'll quit while we're ahead. I've got things that have to be done." What if she asked for examples? Change the cat's whisker on Grandpa's crystal set? Milk the elk?

Leafy kept testing the floor of the trailer with her forefoot, then finally loaded up. Delicate as she seemed to Patrick, the trailer set down on its springs. Panniers, lash ropes, spoilable food, all were piled in the truck.

And now a simple dialogue between the two engine exhausts, G clef by Patrick, revving a bit between ratios as he swung about and headed the rig down the mountain, manifold resonating in the gee-haw of faded romance. One of the West's last and smallest wagon trains, he thought; an observation that exhilarated by its brief coldness and necessary stupidity. The two vehicles separated and headed into the distance.

But by the time he reached the ranch, the phone was ringing and she was asking without any introduction, "What *can* I do? What am I *supposed* to do?"

"I don't know."

"But you just don't do anything you please. Do you?"

"Of course not."

"That's all I wanted to know."

She rung off and left Patrick even less enlightened. He decided that it was partly the phone's fault; that even notepaper was inadequate to such an enigma. He played bebop and cooked Chinese food. It seemed the only answer. He wouldn't see love to its senescence without a middle period.

Then she called again. He was eating a trout, curry and rice invention wrapped in won ton skins and playing the Jazz Messengers so loud he almost didn't hear the phone ring.

"Tio's home. But he's so demoralized, it's not like him."

"I don't know what to say to you."

"I wanted to talk to somebody. He's a sick dog."

"There are bigger things than pairing off," said Patrick.

"Like what?"

"Life and death."

"Take the easy ones, cowboy."

"Well, I asked you to leave with me."

"That's another one. You're going downhill. People promise people, Patrick. How is it with you—strand people with all your speeches? Some of us still own up to the ones we made on homecoming day, for crying out loud."

"That bad?"

"That bad."

"Well, I'm getting off before you ruin my dinner." And he did.

Then, to make up for it a little, he took Tio's stud out to ride in what light was left. His food had begun to digest, and the smell of the horse was obviated by the smell of hoisin sauce and curry. They went up the road, the stud spooking about in the shadows but advancing into new

darkness with the pressure on his sides. A partridge dust-
ing in the pale light went off at an angle, and the stud
watched bug-eyed, side-passing through the spot in the
road just vacated by the bird. My God, what a stupid
bastard, thought Patrick. He once had a farrier who
claimed that the two most ignorant things a man could do
were to refuse to cut a stallion and to turn down a drink of
whiskey. Then Tio's stallion gave out a terrific scream as if
to tell any mares in earshot that he feared no bird. As for
Patrick, his love of Claire kept him, with some struggle,
from acknowledging that the thoroughly faulty Tio was
coming to seem human. It wouldn't do.

And anyway, it wouldn't last; that is, it didn't. Coming
back down the road in nearly complete darkness, past one
small ranch with its generator thumping in the cow barn,
Patrick found it necessary to two-hand the horse once
more, like a colt; his muscles felt short and bunched. If he
could have gotten his head down, he would have bucked.

He took the saddle off, hung the bridle and closed the
stud up when Tio materialized from the next, empty, stall;
he must have been sitting on the feed bunk.

"How'd my stud go?"

"He went all right. We didn't do much."

"I've got a gun."

"Oh, great."

"You can't see it, can you?"

"No. Are you going to threaten me?"

"*I don't know what I'm going to do!* Been made to feel
pretty poorly about myself and that leads direct to your
doorstep."

"May I sit down?"

Tio nodded affirmative, but with a crazy, loose-necked
gesture. Patrick sat on the bench next to his forge, hiking
up on his hands and swinging back onto it. Unconsciously,

he looked about at the things with handles: chisels, screw-drivers, hammers.

"Are you drunk, Tio?"

"No."

"What's the deal?"

"You tell me."

"I don't know what it is."

"Except it ain't right."

"I guess not."

"We go' make it right."

Patrick sighed. "Okay." He guessed he wanted it made right; and he could find nothing actual in this suggestion of gunplay. He didn't think Tio could, either. At the same time, he didn't want to be some dim, surprised bozo who couldn't read the cards and got shot.

"Not like you think."

"Why don't you just get rid of the gun so that we can talk?"

"There's no gun."

"Why did you say there was?"

"I thought it would have a different effect."

"I can see that," Patrick replied.

"Gun's like a big car. Just something to arrive in. Real anger you do in your shirt-sleeves."

Patrick got up, uncomfortable, pulled the lamp on over the forge, took the bench brush and tried to be busy, for Tio seemed to bear real forward motion, anger, humiliation, whatever. It was hard to say.

"Usually I get a nap," said Tio.

"I don't follow."

"A nap. I missed mine today."

"Right . . . ?"

Tio looked dead. "So I'm shot. I gotta go home. I gotta

sleep. The restoration process. Let's pick up where we left off. I'm suckin wind. A big nap will solve that."

"Well, as you wish."

"This is me," said Tio. There when they drove the golden spike, his arms held wide. "Hand in hand with nature. The big snooze."

Patrick discovered where Tio had parked when the Cadillac pulled out, lights high, from between the oldest cottonwoods. He hung his chaps under the yellow bug light and considered: *He missed his nap?*

The other thing is, I've got to get this bad-minded horse back to his owner. Every time I ride that bastard, I feel like a monkey fucking a football. That's not a good feeling. And you don't want to get caught at that.

At evening he was heading for Tio's ranch with the stud behind in the trailer. By the time he went under the big hanging gate, he could see Tio's helicopter, and by the time he got as far as the house, he could see Tio inside the helicopter behind its tinted bubble. Patrick felt nervous about this; but he didn't want the horse around, he didn't want the business connection, and he didn't want the excuse for Tio's visits. Anyway, Tio didn't bother to look up. Patrick could see vaguely that he had the headset on— probably getting a weather report on the VHF.

So he unloaded the horse and led him carefully, thinking at first, This is this canner's last chance to get me; recalling Mary's view that the horse was an instrument of the devil. Leading the horse was like flying a kite: He was just a bad-hearted, bad-minded, uncoordinated canner. And the devil had better instruments.

He put the horse up and stepped out of the stable, a kind of West Coast shack with doors on runners and air-conditioning. Claire was on the porch of the house in her yellow dust-bowl dress, one hand dug into her thick hair.

"Come up here, Patrick!"

"I've returned your horse!" he called.

"I see that!"

When he got to the porch, Claire was shaking and her eyes were drawn inward as though to lengthen their focus to eternity.

"He wasn't any good, really."

"I couldn't get him to do anything. As you can imagine, it's best I return him."

She stared at Patrick and laughed, either ironically or bitterly—stopping him. Certainly nothing was funny at all.

"Can you come in?"

"This is getting crazy. I don't understand. I never have understood."

"Just come in."

Patrick was lost—lost passing into the house, then lost in its rooms, whose opaque human shadows stood sourceless and eerie as the shadows birds cast by starlight. He sensed Claire in her cotton dress no more than he sensed Tio getting his weather forecasts a hundred feet away in an aluminum-and-plexiglass capsule as hermetic and sacrosanct as the Oval Office, Lincoln's tomb, the seal on bonded liquor, virginity.

"Come here to me." She shoved the door closed behind him.

"Claire!"

"Shush!" She seized him hard, and by the time he kissed her throat, it was wet with tears.

He whispered, "What's going on?"

"It's none of your business."

"Is that true?" Patrick asked emphatically. They each seemed to him terrifyingly unconnected.

"That's true. Don't worry about Tio until you go and fetch him." She pulled—or, rather, twisted—him down onto the divan; and she was barefoot.

She said "Baby" and lifted to slide her yellow dress under her arms. Patrick thought, This is as good a place to die as any. He was not so far gone as not to note that the West's last stands were less and less appropriate to epic poetry and murals.

"Should I call you baby too?"

"I didn't mean that. I wasn't calling you baby. That's not what it meant." She was naked now and Patrick awaited a bullet.

"I've got to hear what you meant."

"Last chance."

"Last chance . . . Am I going to get killed at this?"

"I don't see how. *I'm* not going to kill you."

Drawing this particular blank, Patrick, in mortal confusion, made love to Claire, who seemed, spasmodic and weeping, finally more martyred than loved. Patrick heard himself a mile off and incoherent.

Then acknowledgment of everything external moving in upon his consciousness appeared as an ice age. He wasn't a captain or a cowboy. He thought for a moment, literally thought, about what he had set out for; and he knew one thing: he was superfluous.

"Why," he asked, "have we been put up with?"

"By whom?"

"By your husband."

"Ask him. I'm through. But you could ask."

"I *will.*"

"Do."

Tio was dead, exhaust piped into the bubble until the smothered engine quit and Tio went on to the next thing. He hung forward in his harness as though starting the international freestyle; it looked like a long swim indeed. Around his dead face earphones whispered news of a world cracking; but Tio was spared. Lust and boredom provided no such indemnity. It made thrill-killers of nice people.

"Do you think we can fly this thing?"

"Oh, Patrick."

"Are you shattered?"

"Not really."

"Did you love him?"

"Sure."

"I wonder what happened."

"No, you don't."

"I think I really do."

"We fucked him to death."

"Don't talk like that."

"And you thought he was a bad man. You thought if you pushed him hard enough, he'd put you out of your misery, like your sister did for herself. But he wasn't a bad man."

"I mean, is it the main thing to be put out of your misery?"

"Are you miserable?" Claire asked.

"Are you?"

"No. I'm in mourning. I wanted to celebrate it with you before you got miserable again. That part of you deserves to live. The rest should be in there with Tio. You might enjoy him like this." She laughed a high, uncontrolled laugh, one that masked not tears but something wild and unreachable. Patrick felt, as he looked into the bubble, that he looked through the bars of a prison; and that in some terrifying way, the voice of Claire was the bright music of the jailer's keys fading in the corridor.

"Would you like to go back in?"

"I really don't think so."

"Scared."

"Yes."

"All you know is what *I* knew when we went inside before."

"I realize that."

"No guts, no glory," she said.

"I'm not going in with you."

Claire stretched her arms over the plexiglass and stared inside. "I guess if I've done nothing else, I showed one of you how to carry the weight and not go to pieces. I didn't go to pieces. He did and you're about to. I've got this feeling I don't want to lose that. The love was real in each case."

You could see the house in its own lights. It looked like an ad for a paint that was weatherproof and that banished evil. It looked flat.

"Is the love gone?" he asked.

"What if it is?"

"I don't know."

"It's nothing you can do anything with. It makes you go around proving you're not rotten or spoiled by sin— Look at him."

"I thought love was all that mattered."

"Well, it's very nice. Taxes awful high in that neighborhood. You know what I set out to do? In my little quiet way? I set out to have been around."

"Get it done?"

"Well, I've been around."

"You learn anything that could help us? See, I'm real in love with you and I'm sort of stuck."

Claire never seemed morbid, cynical or flippant. Patrick could not see how she had been made into this. Her rakish femininity had first drawn him to her; but now her absolute female power, which men fear will finally be turned upon them, was at hand. He was sure she hadn't wished this or wanted to be competed for. But the two of them had made a major purchase on a long-term plan. She at least acknowledged the cost, while Patrick compressed it to a dead husband. She wasn't being cold; she intended to pay.

"I think you should go in with me."

"Why?"

"For a couple of reasons."

"What are they?"

"One is it will never happen again. We have to give him that."

"And the other?"

"You'll have a real good time."

Patrick went. She made it seem easy.

Had the love been real? Patrick thought so. He never specifically changed his opinion. Too, he gave Leafy to Claire. He must have meant something by that. In life, he later thought, shoot anything that moves. Otherwise, discouragement sets in. Tio at least had gotten the latest weather.

Patrick's grandfather shot the best elk of his life. Patrick packed it out for him and arranged for it to be mounted and hung in the Hawk Bar, the place the old man could see from the window of his apartment.

Patrick and Claire corresponded for some time after he went back into the Army and she returned to her child-hood place at Talalah. Once she sent a picture of herself, but he didn't like keeping it around. After that, the correspondence trailed off.

Anyway, his share of the lease money from the ranch allowed him to buy an old second-story flat in Madrid. He spent all his leave time there. Deke Patwell had it from someone who knew someone who knew someone that he had a woman in Madrid, an American named Marion Easterly; and that when she was with him, he was a bit of a blackout drinker. There were some people in Deadrock who had liked Patrick; and a few of them thought, At least he's not alone.

In any case, he never came home again.

ABOUT THE AUTHOR

THOMAS MCGUANE lives with his family on a cattle ranch in Montana. His principal interests are hunting and riding cutting horses. In prosperous years he takes his family to the ocean and his wife to New York. He is hard at work on a new novel.